DESERVING Grace

written by

C. L. JACKSON

DEDICATION

For King

CONTENTS

ACKNOWLEDGMENTS

Writing a book, particularly the first book, is much more difficult than many realize. And while I spent many a day and night, thinking and writing, and thinking about writing, I would be remiss if I didn't acknowledge those who made it possible for me to complete this project. First, I must give a heartfelt thank you to my husband, Leon, whose eyes still make me weak after thirty years. To my beautiful mother, Olivia J. Love, my first editor and fiercest supporter, thank you for always seeing the best in me. To my father, Albert, who always gives me the best of himself. To all of my family and friends, I thank you. Your unwavering support and love mean the world to me!

A special thank you to the Mastermind Writers Group and Phoenix Rising Entertainment!

PROLOGUE

Kenzo Ausar Dallas watched his wife, Noelle, sleeping in her hospital bed. Relieved that she had finally found rest, he could finally look at her emaciated frame. She was barely 100 pounds now, having lost at least 50 pounds from the chemotherapy that was supposed to save her life. He could finally admit that she was dying. His wife was dying. The cancer had taken its toll on her body, and now they waited. The sterile white hospital sheets washed Noelle's fair complexion out even more. Most of her hair fell out, and what was left was stringy. Not the look of a woman who loved going to the salon. Noelle's weekly hair appointments were legendary. Her full head of luscious brown curls that bounced when she walked was replaced with a few strands of hair. He remembered the tears when the first clump of hair fell into her hands. And he remembered even more that he hadn't grasped the severity of the moment. She was strong enough that she would survive this. When she accepted that the chemotherapy had taken her crowning glory, Noelle learned to wrap and wear turbans like Kenzo's mother, Mbetha, always wore. She even walked a little straighter as if she were trying to give herself the confidence she needed to continue fighting. He would watch her move, slowly and surely, through the house as if cancer was yet another task she was being made to endure, like the laundry or cooking. He hid his tears from her and refused to listen to her serious talk of funerals and testaments.

Now, she looked like a wounded angel, not his vibrant wife of the last eight years. How does a lifetime end in only eight years?

Kenzo sat, memorizing every sound she made, in fear that each sound would be the last. Her breathing was slowing, and she'd stopping speaking days ago. He'd stopped the nurses from any more prodding and poking last week. She'd lost so much weight that nurses needed a child-sized cuff to check her blood pressure. That was the final frontier as far as he was concerned. It was of no use. Everyone knew it. And Kenzo, being aware of the damage he'd done while she was healthy, wouldn't allow her to hurt any further. He would spare them both.

Noelle opened her eyes and stared at him with the same eyes that once held so much love and hope. Kenzo moved his chair closer to her bedside and held her small hand. It was almost childlike now and colder than he'd ever remembered. He reminisced on how Noelle would always remark that she would know his touch anywhere because of his warmth. Some days, he knew, that was the only warmth she would feel. He wondered if she knew he was there now. Would she know his warmth, now?

The quiet hours gave him pause to think about the relationship with his wife. Specifically, how he'd been as a husband. Truth was, Kenzo never wanted to be married. Noelle did. He wasn't ready to be a husband, and truthfully still, she wasn't ready to be a wife. They were both so young. But she'd persisted. All her friends were getting married with big weddings. And she wanted one. They'd dated longer than all her friends, and she was feeling the pressure from everyone. And she, in turn, put the pressure on him. So, he went through it, but he made sure she knew that he wasn't happy about it. It was a mess, he mused. Her resented her, and she resented the fact that he was always angry. There was never a moment when he wasn't punishing her. There were moments when he was mean just to be mean. She covered as best she could, lying to everyone, including herself, that they were blissfully happy. And he would give her fleeting moments of hope that he loved her. And he did love her. He just didn't know how to love her without rage.

Noelle gave him a life he never fully appreciated until this moment. Kenzo knew that everyone hated him now. Her friends and family visited the hospital briefly to say their goodbyes, but few could stay for any length of time because he refused to leave the room. He knew that he didn't give her the cancer, but he'd made her life so miserable that he wouldn't have blamed Noelle if she had welcomed the peace of death. There was no way he would ever be able to atone for hurting her all these years.

Noelle's breathing was steadily slowing, and Kenzo vowed that he would never give his heart to another woman. As far as he was concerned, he would never get involved with another woman again. And if he didn't get involved with a woman, he couldn't hurt her. And he wouldn't lose her. That would be his punishment for all the years he'd hurt Noelle. It was the least he could do.

Noelle opened her eyes as he rubbed her hand, trying to give her a bit of his heat. For a moment, Kenzo saw recognition in her eyes. He was sure she could see into his soul. He kissed her forehead, closing his eyes in prayer, and then kissed her lips softly. Against his lips, she whispered, "Grace." Then, as sweetly as she always had and with the last of her strength, Noelle smiled, closed her eyes, and went home.

Kenzo stood there, still holding his wife's hand, with tears streaming down his face. Noelle was gone forever.

And he was finished.

CHAPTER 1

"What do you mean there's a glitch!" Kenzo bellowed. "This deal has been in the works for months. We break ground in two months!" Kenzo Ausar Dallas was furious, and he was not a man to anger when a deal was on the line. After using a portion of Noelle's life insurance money to start his real estate business, he invested the rest of the funds and established a non-profit in her name to support her favorite charities. The Dallas Group was a commercial real estate development firm, and Kenzo built a reputation for fairness, only resorting to savagery when absolutely provoked. And this deal proved to be one of those times. This project was personal, and he took this glitch personally. Very personally.

His partner, Riley Taylor, calmly took a seat in a leather chair at the desk and waited for Kenzo to calm down. Riley knew that his partner was a bit high strung when it came to their work, but he also knew that Kenzo Dallas was a smart man. He just needed to get the initial anger-filled dramatics out of the way. Riley enjoyed being the bearer of bad news, so he could watch the wheels in Kenzo's head turn when he was solving a problem. It was like watching a craftsman at work, especially when he was fired up like this. This is what made Kenzo successful and both of them rich. Riley swallowed the smirk on his face and waited.

"Well?" Kenzo's irritation was palatable. He had been working on this deal for the better part of eighteen months, and there should be no wrinkles at this point. The Noelle Project, named for his deceased wife, was a mid-scale, open-air mall and re-subdivided neighborhood in the middle of an area that most wrote off as irredeemable. For the last five years, Kenzo bought, demolished, and sometimes rehabbed abandoned properties and existing homes, built playgrounds and cultural centers, and waited until the entire section of Jackson's Harrington Heights was a respectable neighborhood again and still affordable to the area's longtime residents. The shopping center would be the culmination of his strategic revitalization plan. A damn-near completely perfect plan. Like Noelle. Every time they'd driven through the area, she remarked on its promise, on what a revitalization could do for the area and the people who live in it. Perhaps, in redeeming Harrington Heights, he could redeem himself.

There could be no wrinkles at this point. Whoever changed their mind would simply change it back. Period.

Riley crossed his legs, picking imaginary lint from the pants of his Armani suit. "A one Grace Harrington is your problem. Seems as though she has convinced her grandmother not to sell the old homestead."

Kenzo closed his eyes to summon a modicum of control. Hettie Harrington had been a tough cookie to convince that his intentions for the area were honorable. He sat at her kitchen table more times than he had with anyone else. Most early sellers were third generation Harrington Heights residents who either wanted to leave or who wanted better living conditions in the area. But Hattie Harrington was a formidable landowner, and eventually, he convinced her to agree to a 99-year lease of the land when he realized that she would not sell the 40-acre tract of land he wanted outright. He needed her land for the shopping center that would be the final piece of the Noelle Project.

Kenzo opened his eyes, a clear sign to Riley that he should continue.

Clearly amused, Riley said, "Seems Hettie has a granddaughter looking to come home and has convinced her that your project isn't a good investment. From what I gather, she's been working overseas and has just returned to Mississippi."

Without saying a word, Kenzo buzzed his secretary. "Cancel my appointments for the day, Carolyn. And get Marcus Byrd on the line." Kenzo and Marcus went to high school together, and he was now a private investigator with the District Attorney's office. Kenzo leaned his head back to think. Another visit to Ms. Hettie would be necessary, but he needed to contend with this new player in the game.

A few moments later, Carolyn buzzed in, "Mr. Dallas, Mr. Byrd is on the line."

"Kenzo, how are you, man? What's up?

"Need you to find some info for me."

"As always. Whatever you need, you know that."

Kenzo took a breath. "I need you to find out all you can about Grace Harrington. She's Hettie Harrington's granddaughter. All I know is that she's just moved back to Jackson after working overseas. See what you can dig up."

Misunderstanding, Marcus, chuckled. "Well, it's about time you got back out there."

Kenzo rolled his eyes. Riley laughed out loud. He had no intentions of getting involved with any woman. That part of his life was over. He thought he'd made that clear to everyone, but it didn't mean that his family and friends weren't holding out hope. "Nah, man, this is strictly business. Just see what you can find out, okay?"

"Alright. Got you. Call you as soon as I know something."

Kenzo clicked the line.

"What are you going to do? If an old Hettie didn't sell, can you imagine what a young Hettie will be like? Riley asked.

Kenzo shook his head. "Hell, if I know. Let's go, man. I need to drive around to clear my head. Maybe go to the site. Might even drive by Mrs. Harrington's." Kenzo rounded the desk and headed for the door. He looked back at Riley, "You coming?

Riley, on a sigh, rose from his chair, thinking the only thing he could, "This ought to be interesting."

Grace Harrington stood on her grandmother's front porch and let out a much-needed sigh of relief. As much as she loved working abroad for the State Department, she was ready to come home for a while. And coming home meant Mississippi, Jackson, and Harrington Heights. In that order. Her last assignment tasked her very soul. Home was peace, but there was no peace when she arrived. She inwardly cringed at the thought. Mama Hettie had all but signed a good portion of the land away to some real estate developer to build a mall. A mall! On Harrington land. Daddy Mose is surely spinning in his grave, she thought. She was just glad she arrived so she could talk some sense into her grandmother.

She took a sip of her hot tea and let the warmth touch her from the inside out. It had been so long to have a moment to herself, with her own thoughts. She moved to the big swing on the porch and plopped down. From this angle, she could see the street, but no one could see her. Always undercover, Grace? She thought to herself.

As she watched the cars drive by, she thought about the new taskforce she'd be leading in a couple of weeks. Jackson emerged as the hotbed of human trafficking activity in the last few years, and the local police, who had been slow to respond to the threat, were overwhelmed. Many of the girls and women trafficked were African American and Latino, and while some she worked with hated to admit it, race and poverty were major factors. But the intelligence she received suggested that new players were in the game. And they were empire-building. Grace's experience with the sex cartels in Europe and the fact that this was home, made this a perfect position for her. Her last assignment was to infiltrate and destroy a cell in Paris that kidnapped young girls and women to sell to the highest bidders. Virgins and children brought the highest prices. The children. The youngest victim had been three years old. When her team rescued that precious baby, she was near-death from starvation and abuse. Grace fought the emotion of the memory but not the anger. Anger drove her as she worked and kept her focused. That last assignment was most of her life for the better part of four years. Her team took down most of the lower level traffickers, but never got to the main money man. She was determined that this wouldn't happen at home. Not in Jackson. The initial pushback on having a Task Force at all disappeared when they found out she was a homegirl. And she'd gone to high school with a few of the officers assigned to the taskforce. While she couldn't wait to get started, she knew she needed to be completely relaxed and serene with no distractions. She needed these quiet hours on her grandmama's porch.

Being home also meant that she could take care of Mama Hettie, who, if she were honest, didn't need her help but obliged her granddaughter. Lifting her mug to her lips, Grace had to smile before she took a sip. Mama Hettie's rules were crystal clear. Didn't matter that Grace was way past grown. Rules were rules. No staying out past Jimmy Fallon's monologue unless she called and no menfolk in her house. If only she knew, Grace thought. She had no intention of seeing, dating, or anything else after the disaster that was Jaden Burke. She shuddered at the invasion of her peace. Jaden was all charm and light until he didn't get his way. Didn't matter how many times you said "yes," the first time you said "no" he forgot everything before it. He'd wanted to get married, which was fine, but he wanted her to outright quit her job. And when she refused, he threw a class-A tantrum. He apologized, but soon, she realized that it wouldn't work and returned his ring. Grace thought Mama Hettie would be disappointed, but the old woman hadn't said a word when she arrived on her doorstep sans ring and husband.

Grace put her empty teacup down and picked up her book. Reading Michelle Obama's *Becoming* solidified for her that she had done and was doing the right thing. She was ready, more than ever before, to become herself.

And she didn't need a man to do that.

CHAPTER 2

"Girl, the brothers hanging these suits tonight."

Grace laughed at Treasure, her best friend since childhood, who knew how to turn a phrase better than anyone she'd ever met. Treasure owned a high-end boutique frequented by all the society ladies in Jackson—black and white. Her shop, Treasures, sold only the exclusive designer clothing and shoes found on New York and Paris runways. Treasure was the belle of the gala in her silver floor length gown that accentuated every curve she had. As soon as the two of them walked through the door, tongues were wagging. Grace felt pale and downright dowdy by comparison in her subdued navy gown despite its plunging back. She'd chosen a strapless mermaid gown in navy that was daring enough to get more than a few appreciative looks but conservative enough that the elders wouldn't be too aghast. The fitted bodice allowed for a hint of cleavage that she could live with.

Still laughing, Grace weakly admonished her friend, "Down, girl, down. I'm here to enjoy myself. The last suit that turned my head gave me a headache. Let's find our table."

Grace was almost giddy. She had not been to the gala for years, and she quickly realized that it was a proverbial who's who in business, law, government, and education. Jackson's Annual Scholarship Gala to support students at the city's two HBCUs was one of the highlights of the Jackson social calendar. But this was her first time attending and lending her support in person. Usually, she bought a table and donated the tickets to her undergraduate sorority chapter, but this year, she bought two tables. The Advancement officer asked her to share her table with a few local government officials to discuss partnerships and opportunities for student internships, and though she didn't really want to work this evening, she understood the nature of duty and responsibility.

By the time they found the table, Grace and Treasure were punch-drunk. Since only a few people knew she was back in Jackson, many were surprised to see her and stopped her along the way to speak, hug, and welcome her home. Grace didn't know how much she missed southern hospitality until that moment. She finally took note of how beautifully decorated everything was, and it took her breath away. The grand hall had been illuminated with soft lighting from ceiling to the tables like a fairyland. Small strings of lights were placed underneath the sheer tablecloths, and the centerpieces were large hurricane vases with floating candles. Each table had a bottle of red and white wines—complements of a winery in Napa Valley owned by an alumna of the College.

As she looked around and smiled at familiar faces, only one made her stare. Standing near the front of the stage, wearing a tuxedo that seemed tailor made to fit, was the most handsome man she'd ever seen. Grace was spellbound at the sight of him: tall, a smooth shade of chocolate brown, with a neatly trimmed beard. Even from a distance and with a view partially obstructed, she could see that he was well built and gorgeous. Just as she was about to lean over to ask Treasure who he was, he looked directly at her. Grace felt her body warm and her face flush as his deep brown eyes stared back at her with a penetrating glare. She was glad that she was seated, so that no one could see her squirm and squeeze her legs together. She felt her body respond in a way she'd never experienced.

To break the spell of him, Grace looked away. When she thought herself composed enough to look in his direction, he was gone. Relieved, Grace shook her head to rid herself of the vision and the salacious thoughts trying to run through her head. Who in the hell was he? And what was that? Gaining her composure, Grace turned her focus on the conversation of her tablemates and tried, in vain, to forget the sexy stranger that nearly made her lose herself in his eyes. Dazed, Kenzo took a breath as he eased into a seat at his table. As he had been for the past five years, Kenzo's firm had been the leading corporate sponsor of the gala. Riley and his woman du jour of the month were speaking in sensually hushed tones and whispers, causing Kenzo to look away. Normally, Kenzo could tolerate Riley's hyper-sexuality; however, the beautiful woman he'd just seen was still fresh in his mind and Kenzo was not prepared for the visceral reaction he had. Not since Noelle had he felt such stirrings, and he didn't like it one bit. When Noelle died, he vowed that he wouldn't fall in love with another woman and to ensure his resolve, Kenzo avoided the opposite sex like the plague. Everyone around him thought he was still in mourning, which he was, but they had no idea that he planned to live alone for the rest of his life. But this woman's eyes made his body respond in a way that made him remember what wanting a woman was like. Kenzo closed his eyes briefly, and her face appeared before him, doe-eyed, high cheekbones, and a full mouth with succulent lips that just begged to be kissed. And Kenzo hadn't wanted to kiss a woman in a very long time, but this one was tempting enough to challenge his resolve.

For the rest of the evening, Kenzo pretended to be interested in the conversation buzzing around him and the evening's program. He watched the slate of college students tentatively approach the podium and accept certificates and awards, their accomplishments and GPAs rattled off to impress all in attendance and especially donors like him and alumni. He concentrated on the stage while his body was thinking about the woman with the full mouth. Kenzo was so focused on trying not to think about her that he almost missed his cue to approach the stage to award the Noelle Dallas Endowed Scholarship. It was the reality check he needed as to why he was there.

"Tonight, we have Mr. Kenzo Dallas to present the Noelle Dallas Endowed Scholarship Award. Mr. Dallas, would you please come forward?"

Grace watched Kenzo's purposeful strides to the podium. All night she'd tried to forget him, and now he had a name. Kenzo. She felt her face flush even though she tried to be unbothered and stoic—at least in her facial expression. But oh, was she bothered—and hot. Grace realized that she was two tables from the stage and was in the direct eyeline of the podium, so she couldn't deny that he was sexier than any man she'd ever encountered in her life. She felt a twinge of jealousy at the Mistress of Ceremonies when he smiled and gave her a brief hug. Grace didn't understand; she'd never been the jealous type. But she wanted to know what a smile, a touch, a hug, from Kenzo Dallas would feel like. She could only hope that when he spoke, he sounded like a bumbling idiot. Please, Lord, let him be stupid.

God clearly was not answering prayer this evening.

Kenzo Dallas's voice was like silk. And her skin felt every syllable like a caress. She almost forgot to listen to what he was saying. Trying to focus on what he was saying and not just the sound of his voice, she was struck by the love and pain in his voice as he described his late wife's love for her community and her Alma Mater. Grace was mesmerized as she watched him present the College and two students with full tuition scholarships, hugging both. As the event photographer posed Kenzo and the students for pictures, their eyes met. The look he gave her was so hot that she thought she would burst into flames. She felt her nipples tighten and her skin heat as she cursed her body's betrayal. Grace had never experienced such a visceral response to a man, not even Jaden, her fiancé. Kenzo Dallas was deliciously dangerous, and she hadn't even met him yet.

But Lord, help her, when she did.

CHAPTER 3

As she always did when she began a new assignment, Grace stood before the entrance of the building in which she would be working and said a prayer. She thanked God for the opportunity and asked for guidance and protection from dangers seen and unseen. Only then could she take a deep breath and walk through the doors. She'd arrived early so she could have a few moments of solitude before everyone else arrived. She was excited but anxious to get started, meet her new team, and for them to get to know her. Her task force wasn't in police headquarters, but in a newly renovated, historic building in Jackson. Downtown was a ghost town when she left, but now the area boasted new hotels and restaurants. Old buildings like the Standard Life Building had been converted into condos and office space. She requested office space in the Standard Life Building so that she could control access to the task force's sensitive information, not to mention the 24-hour security and the card-access only policy.

Grace realized that she didn't have a chance to appreciate the décor of the building before. When she reviewed the office, she was all business, taking note of security issues, space needs, and basic office set-up details. Now that she had a quiet moment to reflect, she could fully appreciate the marble floors and soft lighting. She was glad that developers preserved the bank of elevators, and she imagined the hustle of businessmen in the 1950s and 1960s, in their black or navy suits, rushing and bustling to work. She smiled. Surely, those white businessmen couldn't imagine that the Standard Life Building would have a new standard now. A black woman working in the building and on the penthouse floor!

Approaching the elevators, she noted the cornerstone marking to her left and stopped in her tracks. There, chiseled in stone, was the one name she'd been trying to forget—Kenzo A. Dallas—listed as one of the developers of the project. As she stared at the stone, she remembered the heat in the eyes of one Kenzo Dallas and was confused by this new intrigue of what the A stood for. *Get it together,* Harrington, she said to herself, shaking her head to clear it of thoughts of the most salacious kind. Grace rolled her shoulders and tilted her head a little higher as she entered the elevator. She entered her keycard into the elevator's panel to express her into the penthouse suite.

When the doors opened to the spacious suite of offices, Grace exhaled, and whispered to herself, "No, they couldn't have imagined."

Grace's assistant, Deloria, had already set up the space for the team. Grace was already impressed with the woman's efficiency. Deloria ordered all the supplies and even set evidence boards and the room to Grace's specifications. Grace walked to her private office in the far-left corner of the suite and looked out of the window. Jackson was growing in so many positive ways. She didn't want these monsters, these bottom feeders to ruin her city. As she reflected, her team started coming in. Most were early, which was a good sign and seemed surprised that she was already there. Grace turned from the window to face them.

Smiling brightly, she started the first meeting with her team as she had so many times before: "Good morning, Team. Let's get started."

The ride to Hettie Harrington's should have been an easy one, but his thoughts kept wavering from the Noelle Project and the woman at the gala. Kenzo hadn't seen her again, which was a good thing. She awakened a desire in him that he long thought dead, but clearly wasn't. He'd been consumed with memories of her eyes staring back at him. The attraction was immediate and all-consuming for the last week. Every time he tried to concentrate on work, he found himself thinking about her eyes and her mouth. Her lips were the most luscious he'd ever seen, and the gloss she wore accentuated the shape of her lips perfectly. Then, there were her beautiful eyes, round, and doe-like. More than once, Kenzo imagined those eyes looking up at him, the taste of her lips, and what she would feel like in his arms. He tried to shake the distraction by visiting Ms. Harrington and getting to the bottom of why she changed her mind about the lease. He had nothing left to offer, but perhaps, lean on her sympathies and explain how vital this project was to the community.

Kenzo gripped the steering wheel of the Mercedes as he made the turn to Hettie Harrington's. He found out that her granddaughter was her pride and joy, and her argument against his project was just as persuasive as his for the Noelle Project. Mrs. Harrington begrudgingly allowed him this final audience but knew that her decision was most likely final. Kenzo timed his meeting with the arrival of this granddaughter of Hettie's who had the nerve to swoop in and derail his project.

For a first day, Grace felt pretty good. The team was a good mix of seasoned cops and tech-savvy newbies. Grace needed both sets of skills, because the battle was in the streets as well as online. That's why early cases had been so hard to close. Sex traffickers were already using technology when the police were treating missing women and children as runaways or domestic issues and still making phone calls and going door-to-door like beat cops. She needed seasoned strategies with 21st century technology to win this war.

But all she wanted to do now was to go home, shower, and get some sleep.

All Grace could say when she saw the car in the circular drive was, "Damn." Grace was too tired to notice the car's make or model. But she knew that when Mama Hettie was hosting that meant she was hosting. There was no earthly way she could excuse herself and retire to her room. Mama Hettie would have a fit! Rolling her shoulders back and pasting on her best southern smile, Grace climbed the steps to the porch.

Immediately upon entering the foyer, she stopped in her tracks. She heard the low tremor of a voice that set her body on fire. It was him! Kenzo A. Dallas, and he was here in her grandmother's house. What in the world?! Grace took a deep breath, placed her purse and laptop bag on the sofa in the sitting room, and quietly approached the dining room where she heard the voices. Thankfully, her grandmother met her entrance.

Hey, baby girl, how was your first day?

Kenzo turned to see "baby girl" and almost choked on his own tongue. There she was. The woman who invaded his thoughts and dreams for the better part of two weeks. She was as gorgeous as he remembered. Composing himself, Kenzo stood as she ventured further into the room. Turning slightly, he offered his hand to her, "Kenzo Dallas. Nice to meet you."

Grace couldn't breathe. She looked at her hand in his and immediately felt warm and tingly all over. Handshake greetings were supposed to be quick, but he was still holding her hand. She peered up at him, "Grace Harrington. It's nice to meet you as well, Mr. Dallas. I believe you were at the Gala a couple of weeks ago, right?" Grace's attempts to play it cool were not lost on him. The sparks between them could have set the house on fire. Kenzo reluctantly let go of her hand, and she suddenly felt the loss of heat. Grace turned to her grandmother as she tried to ignore the feeling of being watched. As Kenzo watched her bend slightly to kiss Hettie on the cheek, he couldn't help but appreciate the beauty of her backside and the sly smirk on Miss Hettie's face.

Giving her grandmother a kiss hello, Grace let her know that her day was good but that she was exhausted. Grace hoped that Mama Hettie would excuse her from further conversation. No such luck.

Her grandmother looked at her for a few seconds before speaking and then threw her completely under the bus. "Grace, Mr. Dallas is the developer I had planned on leasing the land to, but I told him that you had other plans for it now that you were home." Grace's head turned from her grandmother to Kenzo so fast that she thought her head would snap. "Yes, Mama Hettie, I..." Her voice faltered. She was rendered nearly speechless, and she was trying to comprehend Mama Hettie's statement while looking into the most gorgeous set of brown eyes she'd ever seen. The look he gave her was an intense as he had the night of the gala. And he was close enough now that she could pick up his scent. Grace gripped the chair in front of her to steady herself as she tried to finish her sentence.

Kenzo stared at Grace, this gorgeous creature who was the reason his project was in limbo and would destroy all his work. Yet, all he could think about was her mouth, and he felt a desire rush through him that he never experienced. Not even with Noelle. Seeing her at the gala from a distance was one thing, but now she was close enough to touch and taste and smell. Quickly gathering his thoughts, he decided to turn the conversation to business before he made a complete fool of himself. "Ms. Harrington, I'm glad you're here. May we discuss your plans for the land? Perhaps, we can reach common ground with your plans and the existing plans for the Noelle Project?"

"Mr. Dallas, I've just returned home from work, and I'm in no position to discuss my plans for my grandmother's land. Frankly, I'm tired and hungry." She was irritated for two reasons, the first of which was at herself for her reaction to his presence.

"Grace! Where are your manners?" Mama Harrington nearly jumped out of her seat.

Kenzo chuckled. Grace clearly had been gone too long if she thought Hettie Harrington was going to let her get away with that. Hettie Harrington still made men take their hats off inside in her house, in her church, or wherever "inside" was. "Perhaps, Ms. Harrington, since you're hungry, and if your grandmother doesn't object, we can discuss it over dinner."

Kenzo's voice was as sensual as she remembered. *She* was about to object, when Mama Hettie accepted for her.

"That's just fine, Mr. Dallas. I have my mission circle meeting tonight, and I didn't know when Grace would be home. So, we just have leftovers from Sunday dinner." Hettie looked at Grace with a look that said, "Do not embarrass me."

Kenzo could have sworn he saw a smirk on Ms. Harrington's face. Grace's mouth opened and closed twice before she spoke. She was stuck, and all three of them knew it. What she also knew was that there was no way she could sit across from this man at a table. She was barely holding it together as it was.

Through clenched teeth, she muttered, "Fine." To Kenzo, she mustered up a smile as best she could, putting her full southern manners on display, "If you'll give me an hour, Mr. Dallas, I'll be ready."

Checking his watch, Kenzo nodded and quickly added, "I'll run an errand and return at 7. Will that be enough time?"

"Yes, Mr. Dallas, I'll be ready."

Ready for what, neither Kenzo nor Grace knew exactly.

CHAPTER 4

Grace decided that she would treat this dinner as any business dinner she'd had before. She chose a black wrap dress that didn't show too much leg or too much cleavage. Just enough of each. She was a woman, after all. Yet, as she put the final touches on her makeup and dabbed on her perfume, Grace finally accepted that this was no ordinary dinner. The butterflies in her stomach were a constant reminder that Kenzo Dallas, a man who'd been in her thoughts since the moment she laid eyes on him, was picking her up and taking her to dinner. But she also needed to remember that he had an agenda or several.

She would do well to remember that Kenzo A. Dallas wanted something like any and every other man she met.

Kenzo returned to pick her up promptly at seven o'clock as he promised. She was half-hoping he would return disheveled and unhandsome, but that wasn't the case. He'd gone home to change, and change he had. He'd traded in his black suit for a navy one, paired with a crisp white shirt but no tie. Kenzo was the epitome of playboy businessman, and she did a deep inhale when she opened the door. No man should look that good. He was looking at her with hunger and desire in his eyes and Grace reminded herself to breathe.

"Ready, Ms. Harrington?" he said in an almost purr. Kenzo tried to sound professional, but she had awakened all his senses.

Grace nodded, and without a word, descended the porch steps with him. When he opened the door to his Mercedes, Kenzo's scent mixed with his cologne threatened to drive her mad. She slid onto the leather seats with a prayer. *Lord, have mercy.*

The University Club was a seductive choice. Grace had never seen such a beautiful restaurant. Anywhere. The University Club was uber-exclusive, and she was glad she'd dressed appropriately. Atop the Marriot Hotel in Downtown Jackson and only accessible by private elevator, the University Club's rotating floor gave its patrons a view of Jackson's lights for miles. Decorated throughout with dark hardwoods and golden mosaics and with impeccable food, the University Club earned its reputation and its price tag.

Kenzo was mesmerized. Grace Harrington was perhaps the most gorgeous woman he'd ever seen. He'd never had such a visceral, overwhelming attraction to a woman. The perfume she wore was killing his senses, and the dress she wore was sexy though conservative. He stole lascivious glances at her when he thought she wasn't looking, which was most of the time, because she was trying to look everywhere but at him. He decided to engage her a bit more in conversation, as they'd spent the car ride as well as the early part of dinner in awkward silence.

"So, Ms. Harrington, what brings you back to Jackson?" He already knew from Marcus's report, but wanted her to tell him. He wanted to hear the melody of her voice.

Grace took a deep breath before beginning. "I was tired of living and working abroad." She didn't know how much to tell him, but would answer any questions honestly, if probed. "And Mississippi is home."

Kenzo nodded but decided to probe a bit. "I'd heard that you're working with the police department. Is that true?" If Marcus's report was right, and he didn't doubt that it was, Grace Harrington was as badass as she was sexy. A dangerous combination for him or any man who wanted her.

Grace raised her eyebrows as she took a sip of her wine. "You heard that, huh? Well, yes, I'm leading a task force on sex trafficking through Jackson and the Southeast," She watched him closely for his reaction. Seeing none, she continued. "I used to work for the State Department, and my office investigated international sex trafficking." Grace exhaled and waited for his reaction to her disclosure, unconsciously biting her lower lip. She wondered if she had said too much. But this wasn't a date. So, why did his reaction mean so much?

Kenzo looked at the woman before him in wonder. The light from the table's candles illuminated her face, her soft curls framing her features. Kenzo traced the rim of his wine glass with his finger, looking directly at her. Calmly, Kenzo asked, "How did you get involved with that in particular? All the way from Mississippi?"

The incredulous look on his face made Grace laugh. "I majored in political science with an emphasis in international relations. My goal was to become an ambassador with all the perks, you know, fancy parties, cultural events, making peace with countries. But my superiors thought my age and look was perfect to infiltrate a small sex trafficking ring in Paris. I posed as the mistress to a Middle Eastern prince recruiting girls for his harem." Grace rolled her eyes at the memory. "None of the other women in the bureau knew Arabic as fluently as I did and couldn't pull it off. So, my undercover career began." She raised her glass in a mock salute.

For the first time in a long time, Kenzo was in awe. "So, you, a girl from the Great State of Mississippi, who speaks fluent Arabic, went to Paris and posed as a Middle Eastern woman, a mistress, to stop sex crimes in Paris. What did your grandmother say to that?"

Grace laughed out loud at that question. "She has no idea. Mama Hettie doesn't know anything about my undercover work. I want her to sleep at night." Her voice lowered, "Even when I can't." She looked away from him. She'd revealed too much, more than she had to anyone. When she returned her gaze to Kenzo, he was staring at her so intensely that she looked away again. "The last assignment nearly broke my spirit. We'd infiltrated a group of terrorists who sold women and children to fund their operations. You can't imagine what I saw."

Kenzo watched her intently as she talked. Finally, he asked, "But you returned here to do the same work. Didn't you want to do something else, or nothing at all?"

Grace shrugged. "Nothing, I suppose. But when I heard that Jackson had become a major hub, I knew I had to do something. And, frankly, I love what I do." Deciding to change the subject and lighten the conversation as well as learn a bit more about what she *had* been thinking about all day, Grace asked, "What does the "A" stand for?"

Kenzo laughed. He recognized the art of deflection. "Ausar. My mother named me for the Egyptian king. From what I understand, Ausar and his wife, Auset, had such an all-consuming love, that she was able to bear him a child even after his death."

Grace was trying to remain composed as he spoke, but there was something so sexy about his mouth as he spoke, and the flames from the candlelight was making him glow. He looked like an ebony god as far as she was concerned. "After death?"

He continued, "Yes. Ausar was killed by his brother, Set, who dismembered him and spread his body all over the land. Auset found each piece and bound him together for proper burial. Well, she found every piece but one. A very important piece, I might add. His brother threw that in the Nile, and it was eaten, they say, by a fish." Kenzo shuddered. "Can you imagine? Well, as legend has it, Ausar visited his wife in spirit and they conceived a son, Heru. My mother taught African history and folklore for thirty years, so there you go."

Grace prodded a bit more, "So, your first name, has a special meaning as well?"

Kenzo traced his wine glass with his finger again and looked at her long and hard. It's been a long time since he talked about himself so casually with a woman, and he was surprised that he didn't mind talking to Grace. He rolled his eyes to the ceiling in mock annoyance, "Of course. For Dr. Mbetha Dallas, it must be either biblical or African, but she made an exception with my name. It's Japanese. My father is part-African American and part-Japanese, so she relented."

As soon as he said it, she could see the Asian influence in his features. Grace appreciated his high cheekbones and the almond shape of his eyes with growing desire. His voice and the movement of his mouth had captivated her like no other, even Jaden. There was a comfortable silence between them as they stole glances at each other. The waiter returned to fill their water glasses, and the intrusion forced both to look at each other at the same time.

Kenzo looked at the lovely creature across the table. She was nervously nibbling on her bottom lip, and Kenzo's desire was rising to a level he didn't know if he could contain. Suddenly, he felt the urge to kiss her, to nibble on her lips as she was doing, to hold her in his arms. He shifted in his seat, the evidence of his desire making him uncomfortable. He decided that talking business might be the only conversation that would squelch his growing attraction to her, suddenly remembering that she was holding up his project. The Noelle Project. The project that was to honor his wife. Inwardly, he admonished himself. *Jesus, man, what are you doing?*

"So, Ms. Harrington, let's discuss your issues with the lease your grandmother and I negotiated?" He paused and then added, "Before your return." He saw a flash of emotion cross her face. Irritation? Anger? Relief.

Grace paused a moment. "Mr. Dallas."

"Please call me Kenzo."

"Kenzo," she said quietly. A few seconds passed before she spoke. "I was quite surprised when my grandmother told me of your plans. I know the area well, and I'll admit that you've done miracles with eradicating the blight in the area now that I've gotten a chance to see more. But I won't let anyone take advantage of my grandmother. Anyone."

Kenzo was having a hard time focusing on what she was saying. It was as if he'd never heard his name before. He frowned. Did she know her grandmother?

"Take advantage of Hettie Harrington?" He couldn't help but smile. "Seriously, Grace, may I call you Grace? Your grandmother was clear about not selling the land. That's why we settled on a lease. Do you know anything about the Noelle Project?"

"No."

Kenzo told her about the project, including that he chose the area to rehabilitate because of his late wife, Noelle. "Noelle was the sweetest soul. She wanted so much for Jackson and particularly, for Harrington Heights. She thought it could be as trendy, as safe and as beautiful as Belhaven and Fondren. This is for her, and she was the most ethical person I knew. I couldn't have embarked on any of this without integrity and her spirit. Even if I wanted to."

Grace saw Kenzo's features soften as he spoke about Noelle. It was clear that he was very much in pain and perhaps, still in love with her. It shouldn't have but it made him even more handsome. "I can appreciate that Kenzo, but when I returned, I'd hoped to develop the land myself."

Kenzo was incredulous. "What are your plans for development?" He knew that she didn't have any definite plans, just dreams. He watched her as closely as she watched him."

"I want to create transitional housing for abuse and trafficking survivors. A place to renew their spirits. So many women and children don't have anywhere to go, and shelters aren't completely safe. Plus, there aren't the necessary services to help. The work I do forces me to see what needs to be done." Grace took a sip of water, her mouth suddenly dry. Sitting across from him was getting to her, and the longer they sat there, the more she was drowning in his eyes. "And what a lot of people don't understand is how devastating financial abuse can be. A lot of abusers keep their victims financially dependent to make victims feel helpless, or worse, hopeless. It's unreal. And those who have been trafficked have it even worse. Their worth is inextricably linked to their bodies as physical currency."

Grace looked away from him, thinking of one of the first women she'd met on an assignment in Paris. Clarissa. Clarissa had been kidnapped at fifteen and her virginity auctioned on the Dark Web. By the time Grace met her, Clarissa's kidnappers programmed her to believe that her entire sense of worth was her sex. As much as she tried, Grace couldn't get her off the streets. The last time she saw Clarissa, Grace gave her some money, a bible, and a hug. And then she walked away.

Grace felt a tear spring up at the memory, but she didn't want to cry. Clarissa was the rule, not an exception. There were a million Clarissas being trafficked, and to think that it was taking a stronghold at home, was killing her inside.

Kenzo saw the passion and the tears that threatened to fall. "Grace," he whispered hoarsely. When she didn't respond, he called her name again and reached across the table for her hand. Suddenly, he needed to touch her, to feel her skin. As soon as his hand found hers, he felt a surge of protectiveness and concern that, even in the midst of her sadness, made him want to comfort her.

Grace stared at his hand atop hers for a few seconds before she looked up at him. He'd never know what that touch meant to her. Jaden never asked, or pretended to care about her work, or even what she could tell him. It was all too depressing, he'd said. Yet, she could feel Kenzo's heart in his touch, in the way he'd called her name to bring her back from her memories. It was as if he *knew* where she'd just been in her mind. She knew she should move her hand from beneath his, but she couldn't.

"You've seen a lot, haven't you?"

Grace nodded, afraid that if she spoke, the tears would fall.

Still holding her hand, Kenzo stood and she rose with him. "I think it's time to go." Kenzo liked the feel of her hand in his, and he liked even more that she didn't pull her hand away. He led her to the elevator without another word. Once in the elevator, he pulled her closer to him. Kenzo felt her body relax, and he felt a sense of pride that he was able to do that for her. He wanted to kiss her, to feel her lips against his, but decided against it. He didn't want to be selfish. He knew what selfishness could do.

Grace didn't know exactly what was happening between them, but she didn't care to think. She just wanted to feel, and Lord knows, Kenzo Ausar Dallas felt good. His touch was sending electric pulses throughout her body, and she felt her body heat. She peered up at him and wondered what he was thinking. She knew what she was thinking. She desperately wanted to be kissed and kissed by him.

Kenzo and Grace rode in companionable silence. Grace didn't ask where they were going, and he didn't offer an itinerary. Kenzo's hands were gripping the wheel, and Grace used her vantage point to take stock of him. Her gaze drank him in from the strength of his hands to his broad shoulders. He'd taken off his suit jacket, so she was able to see the thickness of his biceps under his shirt. His jawline was strong, chiseled, with a well-trimmed beard. His profile was just as sexy as the rest of him.

Kenzo pulled into an open tract of land in Harrington Heights. Turning to Grace, he said, "We're here. There's something I think you should see."

Grace immediately recognized her family's land. Was all of his concern just a ruse to get her defenses down? Grace frowned and crossed her arms. "Why are we here, Kenzo?" She was hoping that it wasn't what she thought, because it would definitely damper her thoughts of him.

"I think you need to see something." Kenzo got out of the car and walked to the other side to open her door. Her arms were still folded, and the act of defiance pulled his eyes toward the roundness of her breasts. When he extended his hand, Kenzo wondered briefly if she would take it. She stared at his hand and up at him, the look of confusion, hurt, and need on her face let him know that she didn't understand. "Please, Grace, come with me. Just for a moment. We won't be here long."

Reluctantly, Grace took his hand and surrendered to its warmth. She and Kenzo walked further in the field before he spoke. He decided not to sugarcoat anything and just tell her the truth.

"I wasn't a good husband, Grace. To tell the truth, I was horrible, and I made her life miserable. And there wasn't time for me to make amends. The Noelle Project is my apology but her brainchild. This is really her vision, and when I heard you talk about your work and what you wanted to do here, I knew, Grace, that Noelle would love to be a part of something like that. She'd probably be your first volunteer." Kenzo suddenly became aware that he was still holding Grace's hand. Somehow, Grace's hand in his gave him strength.

Grace listened intently. It was the same pain she'd heard the night of the gala. She waited for him to continue.

"Noelle hated the blight in Harrington Heights. She saw it all. I laughed at her vision. So, when she died, I vowed that I would be the man she thought me to be. This is all her. Not me. I was even determined that I wouldn't get involved with another woman. I couldn't bear the thought that I would hurt a woman like I hurt her."

"You haven't been...involved?" He turned to her, knowing what she was asking.

"No. I threw myself into my work. I threw myself into this project."

"I'm sure she didn't expect this for you."

"No, but she always let me figure things out in my own time. I just ran out of time before I figured things out with her." Kenzo took a deep breath.

"Kenzo, why are you telling me this?" She held her breath.

"Because I want you to know that I understand how memories and purpose are linked. Whatever and whoever you were thinking about at the Club touched you, and I wanted you to know that this isn't just business with me. It's personal."

Grace nodded as she looked around the land. The moon was full and bright, and the lushness of the grass beneath her feet made her proud to be a Harrington. It was as if she could feel Daddy Mose's presence here, as the memories of her childhood flashed before her. And then she looked at Kenzo. His almond eyes were searching hers. "Will you give me a few days, Kenzo, to think about all you've said."

"Of course." He squeezed her hand. Let me take you home. I don't want Miss Hettie angry at me for keeping her granddaughter out past a respectable time. That's the last thing I need in my life."

They burst into much needed laughter on their way back to the car.

CHAPTER 5

Kenzo didn't hear a word Riley said. After three days since his dinner with Grace, his nights were spent in utter torture, remembering her scent, the movement of her mouth when she spoke, the way she licked her lips and closed her eyes in appreciation of her food, and even her strength when she tried to hide her tears from him. And most of all, his memory of her hand in his made him squirm in his seat, even now. He still remembered the softness of her skin against his and how it brought out this protective streak in him as if she was his responsibility. But she wasn't his responsibility. He had his chance to care for a woman, and he wouldn't have the chance again.

Riley closed his portfolio and stared at his partner. "Kenzo, have you heard anything I've said for the last hour?"

When Kenzo looked at him blankly, Riley continued. "I said that the property on Livingston near Five Points is up for auction. Shame that the owners didn't take the buyout you offered last year. Auction is scheduled for Friday. You want me to handle it?"

"Yeah, man, you can handle it. Don't go over $40,000 though."

"Cool. What's with you. You've been zombified for the last three days."

"Zombiefied?" Kenzo chuckled. "You kept your nieces and nephews last weekend, I see?" Riley, ladies' man that he was, loved his nieces and nephews and often kept them at his home to give his sisters a break. His sisters, Rachel and Chloe, had two a piece, each a boy and girl, around the same time. Keeping them on a regular basis was great birth control.

Kenzo shuffled the papers in front of him, refusing to look directly at his friend. "Nothing's up. Just been distracted lately. No big deal."

Riley watched his friend. He knew better. "Wouldn't have anything to do with a certain woman you took to the University Club a few nights ago, would it?"

Kenzo glared at Riley. Of course, it was, but he wasn't going to admit it. "How in the hell?"

"Jackson, man. You can't do anything in this city that folks won't find out about. So, who was she?" Riley was one of the few people who knew Kenzo's self-imposed purgatory since Noelle's death. If Kenzo was seen on a date with a woman, it meant something.

"Grace Harrington." Kenzo looked at Riley with as much a deadpan look as he could muster.

"Hettie Harrington's granddaughter?"

"One and the same. It was a business dinner. I wanted to talk to her about that tract of land she didn't want to lease. But..."

"But what?" Riley sat up a little straighter and watched Kenzo relive it all. He knew that his friend was going through something major.

Kenzo's expression was one of defeat. "Man, I don't know what happened. One minute, I'm sitting at Miss Hettie's table, then next I'm inviting her to dinner. And then, once we were there and got to talking, I started enjoying myself too much. I even took her to the site after."

"Did y'all?

Kenzo cut him off before he could finish the sentence. "Hell, no. You know my position, Riley."

"Look, Kenzo, it's been five years. No one would blame you. And Noelle wouldn't want this for you. But I know this, she must be one helluva woman to make you zone out like this. So, are we getting the land or what?"

"I don't know. I haven't talked to her since that night. But I did ask her to think about it. She said she would. Guess I should call her."

"You think? You have been out of the game too long if you haven't called her in three days. You're wasting time."

Both Kenzo and Riley knew how loaded that last statement was, and Kenzo knew he was right.

"Alright, man. I'll call her today."

———

Grace was reading her latest report on the most recent trafficking cases. Her team worked well together. She decided that their first order of business would be to gather as much intel on the known criminals in the area engaged in interstate trafficking and the local pimps in the area. Some of the names were familiar because they were local, but there were a couple of surnames that were giving her pause.

She thought of her new team. Different from her last group, but just as dedicated. She and Zara Bailey were the only women on the team. Zara was young and up on all the latest technology. She was even teaching Grace some new things. Grace smiled. Zara reminded her a lot of herself early in her career, but Grace could tell she wanted out of Jackson. Grace understood that completely, but she also knew that Zara would eventually miss Jackson as much as she did.

The other members of the team, Luther Paige, Terry Gates, and Edward McDaniel were highly decorated detectives in the Jackson Police Department. While the men were all top-notch, only McDaniel worried her. He seemed more interested in the pursuit than the details, but he was still young. Perhaps, he hadn't seen enough. She knew Luther and Terry from high school, and initially worried about whether they would be able to follow her command, but so far, they hadn't had any problems.

She was deep in thought when her intercom buzzed:

"Ms. Harrington, Mr. Kenzo Dallas is on line one."

Grace stared at the intercom like it would bite her. She tried for three days to forget she knew that name. She was a master at compartmentalization. In her line of work, Grace found that hardline separation kept her focused, but the memory of him was trying her very soul.

After a moment, Deloria's voice brought her to her senses. "Ms. Harrington? Would you prefer that I take a message?"

"No, thanks, Deloria, I'll take the call."

Grace took a deep, calming breath, and picked up the receiver. "Grace Harrington."

Kenzo's rich voice seemed to float through the phone. "Hello, Ms. Harrington. How are you?"

Grace felt her entire body respond to his voice. She felt her cheeks flush and her skin heat. "I'm well, Mr. Dallas. I bet I know why you're calling. You want to know if I've decided to lease the land to your company."

"No, I called to see if you'd like to meet for lunch. And please, call me Kenzo."

Grace smiled. "I don't know, Mr. Dal...Kenzo. I have a great deal of work to do."

"But you do have to eat, right?"

Hesitantly, Grace agreed, "Well, yes, but..."

"Well, then, it's settled. I'll meet you in the lobby in fifteen minutes. Agreed?"

"Yes, Kenzo, agreed." Just before hanging up, Grace had a thought. "Wait!"

"Yes, Grace."

"How did you know where I was. I never gave you my office information."

"This is Jackson, Love. Welcome home. See you in fifteen." He was laughing as he hung up the phone.

Grace gasped slightly at the term of endearment. She'd never been into such affectations. Jaden always called her Grace, and she by his name. But the richness of Kenzo's voice washed over her, but she knew she needed to get herself together if she was going to see him again. She'd given considerable thought to the lease and had some plans she wanted to discuss. Perhaps, this would be the last time she would be subjected to the sexiest man she'd ever met. She had way too much at stake to be distracted by Kenzo Ausar Dallas.

But Lord have mercy...Grace laughed to herself as she fanned herself in a mock swoon. She needed to speak to Treasure and grabbed her cellphone.

Treasure answered with her usual ebullience. "Hey, girl!

"Treasure, he called today and asked me to lunch."

"Kenzo? Chile! After three days?" Treasure paused and Grace was silent.

"Should I go? I don't have time for distractions."

"Of course, you should go, and you will go. And girl, we should all be so lucky to have such a scrumptious distraction. You know what I would do! First, though, you need to rake him over the coals for waiting this long to call you. And then, order the most expensive thing on the menu."

"Girl, you are crazy! Bye!"

"So, you're going? We both knew that you were going. You just wanted me to cosign it. Have fun and I want all the details this evening."

"Bye, Treas. Thanks."

She grabbed her purse and informed Deloria that she would be back in a couple of hours. Headed to the elevator, Grace found herself smiling.

Exactly fifteen minutes later, Kenzo was waiting for Grace to exit the elevator. He saw her before she noticed him. She was simply beautiful. She was wearing a navy-blue dress that showed off her toned and shapely legs. Kenzo felt a surge of desire sweep through him. But when he watched her speak to everyone in her path from other businessmen to the security guard, he could see the genuineness in her smile. Grace Harrington was simply breathtaking. He approached her while she was speaking to a young lady on the custodial staff.

Grace felt him before she saw him, and her suspicions were confirmed when Tiffany stopped talking in mid-sentence.

"Grace."

Grace turned around slowly. Every time he said her name it was like she'd never heard it before.

Tiffany spoke before she did. "Hi, Mr. Dallas, how are you?"

"I'm well, Tiffany. How are the boys?"

"Doing great. Joshua is playing baseball, and Jeremiah is growing way too fast."

"I'll come check on them soon."

"Thanks! They'll love that! Well, see y'all later. Got to get back to work." Tiffany left them standing there facing each other.

Grace watched the exchange between Kenzo and Tiffany without a word. She was intrigued but was trying to deal with the twinge of jealousy she felt at the familiarity between them. Their rapport didn't seem sexual, but Grace still felt territorial despite knowing she had no right to be.

Kenzo smiled. "Ready to go?"

Grace nodded, "Yes, where are we off to this time?"

"Well, since you're so busy, I thought we could have lunch at my office." Before she could respond, Kenzo placed his hand in the small of her back, leading her toward the elevators. He led her to the last elevator and used a black key card to open the doors. Once inside, he swiped it again and pressed 25.

As the elevator ascended, Grace admitted her confusion. "I don't understand. Your office is in the building?" *Lord, have mercy,* she thought. *This is more than a distraction. This is suicide.*

"Yes, my partner and I were part of the redevelopment. I've already ordered. I hope you don't mind, but I think you'll be pleased. It should be delivered shortly." Grace's intoxicating scent was filling the elevator, and Kenzo was getting high from it. His hand was still tingling and warm from touching her back. It was as if he could still feel her heat in his palm. She must have felt something too, because she gasped at the contact. The ride was swift but so electrically charged that Kenzo wondered if this lunch was a good idea. His resolve was being tested like never before. He'd never been this interested in a woman, and since Noelle's death, it was safer to just remove himself from the dating scene. But Grace Harrington made him think, and now, he was doing things he hadn't allowed of himself in five years. Grace was igniting pieces of him that he buried a long time ago.

The elevator doors opened to his office suite, and both Kenzo and Grace hesitated before stepping out of the elevator. Kenzo placed his hand on the small of her back and nudged her forward. He heard her small gasp as a current passed through them. He watched her slowly move forward into the office's reception area, and from a remote place in his mind, he heard the elevator doors close. But Kenzo's focus was solely on the woman before him.

He gathered his thoughts enough to introduce her to his assistant, Carolyn, who let him know that the food had arrived, the conference table was set, and the Harrington folder was on his desk. As Carolyn talked, Grace hung back, her posture as business-like as possible, yet, he couldn't help but notice a slight frown crease her brow.

Kenzo headed for his office, and Grace followed. Kenzo could barely think to put one foot in front of the other, glad that he was in front of Grace. He didn't think he could handle watching the natural sway of her hips right now. As conservative as her dress was it couldn't mask natural curves, and Grace possessed all of the curves that mattered to a man. For a spilt second, Kenzo second-guessed his decision, but this inexplicable need to be near her was driving him forward. Grace's scent was as intoxicating as it had been three nights ago, and he knew that it would be his undoing.

Grace took a moment to really take everything in. Knowing that he was in the same building was unnerving. Another distraction Kenzo Ausar Dallas presented. Their suites were nearly identical, but she was impressed that whoever decorated was good, blending traditional and modern furnishings. The large antique desk worked extremely well with the chocolate leather chairs for guests. The conference table was antique as well but didn't overpower the space. But Grace was spellbound by the artwork. The walls were adorned with cultural art from Jackson to the Mississippi Delta Blues Festival and even a few African sculptures. There was even room for a small leather love seat that matched the chairs at his desk. The loveseat was accented with red throw pillows and looked perfect for snuggling. Snuggling with Kenzo. Grace took a cleansing breath and shook her head. *That is not what this is, Grace. This is lunch. He wants something. Remember that.*

Against her better judgment, Grace turned to face Kenzo. "Nice office."

Kenzo smiled at her, and she felt her entire body respond to him. She felt heated but her body shivered. His smile ought to be outlawed, she thought, as she closed the distance between them. He may want something, but Grace realized she wanted something too. "Thanks, I hired a decorator, but she knew what I liked."

"She?" Grace didn't understand her second twinge of jealousy she'd felt that day.

"Yes, Kenya Jones, she was a sorority sister of Noelle's." Quickly changing the subject, Kenzo asked, "Ready to eat?"

He was setting the table in the breakfast nook, but he must have sensed her, because he looked up and their eyes met.

She returned his smile with one of her own, determined to get her raging hormones under control. "Smells good. What did you order?"

"Well, I know Ms. Hettie can throw down, but I remember you saying that you missed soul food while you were abroad and one place in particular."

Grace looked at the spread of soul food. She groaned in horror. "You didn't. God, no. I won't be able to work this afternoon."

Kenzo laughed, and Grace liked the sound. He hadn't laughed much when they ate dinner at the Club, so this was a welcome change. It looked like he'd ordered everything on the menu, and the aromas of oxtails, greens, mac and cheese, and pork chops filled her nostrils as she took a seat.

Kenzo reached for her hand and when she placed her hand in his, he bowed his head and said a blessing over the food. In that moment, Grace knew she was a goner. Full swoon alert. When he finished praying, Grace couldn't help herself and asked. "You didn't pray at dinner. Why now?"

Kenzo paused, "Grace, this isn't business. I had a good time the other night. Maybe too good." He stopped again, this time with a shy smile. Grace inwardly sighed, trying not to fall into the depths of those gorgeous eyes staring back at her. "And I hoped that we could get to know each other. Become friends. And with my friends, I'm honest about who I am and what I believe."

Grace had never felt faint before and especially over a man. But Kenzo invoked emotions in her that she didn't recognize. He sounded so sincere that he didn't sound real. But, somehow, she knew he was being real, but she needed to know before she went any further. She remembered that Carolyn mentioned the 'Harrington folder.' "Are you sure you want to become my friend, or is this because you want me to sign the lease for Mama Hettie's land?" There. She'd said it. Grace looked at him expectantly, waiting for him to answer, hoping that she wouldn't detect one ounce of bull. This was a moment of truth, and Grace knew that this would be the turning point for her. Either he would tell her the truth, or he would lie to her face. She would know either way.

Kenzo calmly returned his fork to his plate. He couldn't blame her for asking the question. He looked directly in her eyes—beautiful brown eyes that he noticed, at that moment, had flecks of green. She went completely still, waiting for him to answer.

For a reason he couldn't understand, in this very moment, he wanted to be completely honest with Grace. "Grace, after my wife's death, I vowed to be completely honest with my emotions, because I spent too much time pretending. Let me be clear, Grace. I'm attracted to you, and I think you're attracted to me. I have been since the gala and that was before I knew you were Hettie Harrington's granddaughter. So, the land has nothing to do with this, whatever this is, happening between us."

The intensity of the look shared between Kenzo and Grace seemed to electrify the room, and they resumed eating. Grace savored each delicious bite of her meal from the oxtails to the greens. She didn't know how she was going to eat the peach cobbler, but, damn, if she wasn't going to try. Eventually, they started talking, small talk at first, but then she decided to let him know her plans regarding the land.

"Kenzo, I'd would like to talk to you about the land. I really have thought about what you said the other night. And I do appreciate you taking me to it. It brought back such memories. Good memories that reminded me of why I came home." Grace paused. She couldn't read Kenzo's face.

"Grace, we don't have to do this now. I was being honest earlier."

"I know you were, and that's why I've decided to tell you my decision. Or at least give you a proposal."

Kenzo found himself laughing. "You definitely are Hettie Harrington's granddaughter."

Grace smiled, and Kenzo thought it was the most beautiful smile he'd ever seen. Her face lit up.

"That I am. I'll tell Mama Hettie to sign the lease on one condition. I would like space for a transition workforce center and small business incubator for survivors. If you sell the property, then I need that as part of the deal for the term of the lease."

"You have thought about it." Kenzo was impressed with Grace's forethought. Her eyes were focused and narrowed as if she were poised for a fight. Kenzo and Grace stared at each other for a moment. In negotiations, Kenzo never acquiesced. He normally had worked through all of the options before even sitting down to the bargaining table. Any concessions his opponents thought he made were already worked into his plans. But this woman was unlike any opponent he'd faced. Kenzo knew he would give this woman anything she wanted. And the thought scared him and comforted him at the same time. He could tell she'd become tense again.

"Yes." Grace knew that it was a lot to ask, and she really had no right to ask. After all, Mama Hettie was the sole owner, and somehow, she knew that her grandmother would eventually sign the original lease. Mama Hettie liked Kenzo and had told Grace many times since his visit to the house three days ago. Just three days? Grace began to worry that he wouldn't agree to her terms, but she wouldn't budge.

Kenzo rose from the conference table and put both of their empty plates into the garbage without another word. When he returned to the table, he stood by Grace's chair and extended his hand. She found herself rising and following him to the loveseat. Kenzo motioned for her to sit. Grace couldn't understand why she easily followed him. It was as though she was entranced. Kenzo turned slightly to her and she did the same.

"Grace, as I told you the other night, the Noelle Project is the brainchild of my late wife. She had a vision of renewal and rebirth for Harrington Heights, so yes, I will agree to your proposal. I'd like to check with the attorneys to see if we can demand space 'in perpetuity.' But whatever I can do to make it happen, I will.

Grace nodded and a sudden urge of desire filled Kenzo like never before. Kenzo felt the air surrounding them crackle, and he knew he needed to taste her. "Grace. I need to do something I've wanted to do for the last three weeks." The intensity of Kenzo's stare made her feel like prey. And for once, Grace didn't mind getting caught. Without another second, Kenzo cupped her face in his hands and kissed her. It was the sweetest kiss. She heard a moan and realized that it was her. Kenzo deepened the kiss and captured her tongue and manipulated it in ways she'd never known was possible. It was as if he was making love to her mouth, and Grace was burning up with desire. Her nipples swelled against her bra and her skin warmed with his touch. She felt flush and knew she was drenched. She couldn't go back to work after this. But she couldn't stop herself. He was devouring her mouth and she was devouring his. Grace had never known such heat. She returned his passion, and Kenzo pulled her closer to him so she could feel the effect she was having on him.

Kenzo was losing control of his senses. The intoxicating smell of her arousal had invaded his nostrils, and he couldn't stop kissing her if his life depended on it. When she nibbled on his bottom lip, he had moaned out loud.

Kenzo could tell that she wanted him as much as he wanted her, but he couldn't make love to her now. Not like this. He had to summon some control, yet her taste, her scent were driving him insane. He held her tightly with one hand while the other was teasing her thigh. He needed to stop this before it went too far.

Reluctantly, he pulled away and placed his forehead on hers.

"I don't know what you're doing to me, Grace," he whispered. He looked at her and resisted the temptation to kiss her again. "Do you need to get back to work?"

Grace took a deep breath. Yes, it had been two hours since she left the office. She needed to get back, but she didn't know how she could go and sit at her desk. Not after this kiss. "Yes, I do," she said quietly. "May I use your restroom?" Grace needed space from him for a few moments. When she closed the door, she leaned against it, her body still recovering from his kiss and her loss of control. As she brought her breathing under control, she looked at her flushed face and swollen lips in the mirror. She was glad she kept a bag in the office with a change of underwear, because these were through. When she felt ready to face him, she left the bathroom. He was standing in the middle of his office, and as if he sensed her presence, Kenzo turned around. He approached her with concern in his eyes

"Will you have dinner with me tonight?" He looked at her with pleading eyes.

Grace's heartbeat jumped. Kenzo had become more than a mere distraction and she should say no. But she couldn't. She looked at the couch and the memory of what just happened between them flooded her senses.

"Kenzo, I...

"Just dinner. I promise."

"Just dinner?"

"Scout's honor."

"Then, yes, I'll meet you for dinner."

"I'll walk you to your office."

"No, please. I can manage." She didn't want Deloria or any of her team to see them together. It would be obvious that they did more than eat lunch. She said a quick prayer of thanks when Carolyn wasn't back either. She picked up her purse and headed to the elevator. Once inside, she stopped for a moment. Maybe this wasn't a good idea. "Kenzo, maybe..."

Kenzo knew she was about to cancel. He couldn't let her do that. "I'll pick you up at 8."

And with that, Grace watched the elevator doors close on Kenzo's parting smile.

CHAPTER 6

Grace was facing the large board in her office. She and her team placed the major traffickers' pictures and traced their connections on the board to have a visual of the evil as much as to see how all of the players were connected. Some were low-level pimps in Jackson, but even they were getting into some trafficking action—too stupid to know that they would be sacrificed to protect the game's big men. She'd learned a long time ago that if you follow the streets, you'll just get the trash. But if you started big, then you could topple the entire organization.

"Are we sure that these are all of the players? Because when this thing gets started, I don't want any loose ends."

Zara was the first to speak up. "From the interviews and police reports, these are all the names we could gather."

Grace turned from the board and faced the team. "Then, that's the problem. I want the names that they are afraid to say out loud." The determined look in her eyes said she meant business, and her team was prepared to follow her in that moment. "Luther, Terry, see what your CIs can give you. Lean on them. All confidential informants have a weakness. Exploit it." Grace turned to Zara and Edward. "I need a list of every trafficking transaction on the Darknet for the last year between Texas and Florida. We'll expand it if necessary."

"Sure, Boss," said Edward, "but that may take time we don't have."

"It won't take as long as you think. Plus, we're going to work the streets at the same time. And if I need to expand our group, I have authority to do so. But I want to wait until we have more information. Remember, we're not looking for quick wins but long-term results. Good work today. See you guys tomorrow."

With the team gone, Grace kicked off her heels and plopped in her chair. Getting the board and making the connections between criminals was always taxing, but Grace couldn't shake the feeling that she was missing more than a few links. And there was one perp that looked familiar, but she couldn't place the face. But she knew that they were still gathering intel, so she wasn't going to worry.

What she needed to worry about was Kenzo. And what she was going to do about him. She tilted her head back, the memories of the night before flooding her. Grace still couldn't believe how far she'd let things go with Kenzo. Even now, she remembered everything that night as if it was playing like a movie before her.

Kenzo took her to another expensive and intimate restaurant. Candlelit. He'd arranged for a private room, giving them complete privacy. He looked more gorgeous in a dark gray suit with a lilac shirt than any man she'd ever seen. Grace was glad that she'd chosen her green dress. The coloring of the dress completed her skin tone and accentuated her curves. She knew she'd made the right choice from his open appraisal of her when he arrived at Mama Hettie's. The food was amazing, but the conversation was even better. They laughed and joked about their childhood, and she even told Kenzo about the time Mama Hettie whipped her within an inch of her life for going to the store without permission. He told her some of his 'bad boy' stories. And Grace believed them all. She could sense that the polished businessman before her was passionate and sensual, if that earlier kiss was any indication, who could be deliciously bad.

After dinner, Kenzo ordered dessert to go even though she tried to beg off. "Kenzo, after lunch and dinner, I can't bear to eat another bite." He flashed her a devastating smile and said nothing. They stared at each other for a few minutes, the sexual chemistry between them palpable. Grace was glad that they were in a semi-public place, because, private room or not, the sparks between them were threatening to ignite. When the waiter returned, Kenzo took the doggy bag and paid the check, looking at her the entire time with such an intense look that Grace unconsciously took a step back.

They drove around the city for an hour. Kenzo pointed out the new construction projects around town, some of which he was involved in, new subdivisions, and shopping centers. Jackson didn't have a movie theater anymore, so he told her of his plans to build a state-of-art entertainment complex near her Alma Mater. Grace listened to the passion in his voice as he talked about making Jackson the new Atlanta, Houston, or Dallas. She had no doubt that he could do everything he wanted to do. It made her want him even more. Grace realized during dinner that Kenzo was quickly working his way past her defenses.

She was so busy focused on him that she was caught off-guard when the car stopped. Kenzo turned the engine off and shifted in his seat to face her.

"I thought we could come here, to my home, for dessert. And before you say it, I didn't bring you here for any other reason than I just don't want the evening to end." In his soul, Kenzo knew that he was taking a major step. Though it wasn't the home that he'd shared with Noelle, this was the first time that a woman, other than family, had been there. As he waited for her to respond, Kenzo gripped the wheel.

Grace touched Kenzo's arm. She felt his muscles relax at her touch. "I don't want it to end either. And now, I'm ready for dessert." Grace and Kenzo's eyes met. The double meaning of her words wasn't lost on either one of them.

Grace didn't know what she expected, but this certainly wasn't it. Kenzo's home was simply breathtaking. Once past the threshold, Grace entered a spacious foyer that led into a spacious great room. The foyer's beautiful red walls transitioned into a beautiful oatmeal color. Both colors were perfect complements to the rich, cherry hardwood floors. Like his office, he'd adorned the walls with Asian, African, and contemporary artwork as well as the furnishings from the antique settee to the African masks and sculptures. But the real focal point was the wall of windows that provided an excellent lakeside view. She walked to the windows and looked out at the water.

"Kenzo, your home is beautiful. This view is amazing."

"You haven't seen all of it, but then, I'm not completely finished with the upstairs. But I can take you on a tour of this floor." Kenzo showed her the state-of-the-art kitchen, beaming with pride when she recognized the La Cornue range.

"A La Cornue! Kenzo!"

He laughed at her excitement. "You cook?"

Grace rolled her eyes. "Yes, I can cook. Just because you've fed me all day doesn't mean I can't cook. Baby, I can throw down." Grace snapped her fingers for effect. "Lord, I could cook all of Thanksgiving at one time with this baby. But it's so expensive, I could only dream of owning one."

"Well, now you can cook on this one. Anytime."

"Don't threaten me with a good time, Kenzo." If I start cooking in this kitchen, you'll never get me out of here." Grace was laughing, and Kenzo realized how much he liked her laugh. How at ease with her he felt. And more than anything, he realized that yes, he wanted her cooking in this kitchen because she seemed so happy to do so. He'd tried those traditional ideas with Noelle, who eventually resented the expectation despite wanting to cook. He shook his head to rid himself of the memory.

"I'll even let you cook Thanksgiving. Come on, let's finish the tour...such as it is." Kenzo grabbed her hand, feeling the current pass through them. He took her to the sunken den, where he spent most of his downtime. His baby, the 80" flat screen, was hung on the wall. It was a completely decked out man cave, complete with a huge sectional couch, fully stocked bar, and sports memorabilia collection.

Grace burst into laughter. "Of course. Now this is what I expected."

Kenzo feigned hurt, giving her his best Fred Sanford impression, which made her laugh even harder. As he doubled back to the kitchen to grab the dessert, Grace's laughter was still ringing in his ears. He stopped short when he saw her on the couch. Grace kicked off her shoes and tucked her feet beneath her. Her dress revealed more of her thigh, and he imagined how soft they would feel to the touch.

"Hungry?"

"Very."

He sat next to Grace, his knee touching hers. She felt his heat even with that small bit of contact. He opened the box to reveal the restaurant's award-winning turtle cheesecake with caramel sauce. Kenzo made a grand display of pouring the hot caramel sauce on the cheesecake, and Grace thought it was the sexiest thing she'd ever seen. She licked her lips in anticipation, but even she couldn't tell if she was thinking about the cheesecake or Kenzo. Kenzo fed her the first bite, and she moaned loudly in appreciation. He watched Grace lick a bit of caramel that lingered on her lips. He was instantly aroused by the sight and the memory of her taste from their earlier kiss. Kenzo fed them both, and when he gave Grace the last bite, he knew he had to kiss her again.

Without a word, Kenzo placed the empty take-out container on the coffee table, never breaking eye contact with Grace. He allowed his gaze to roam over her body, resting briefly on the swell of her breasts, before rising to meet her eyes. He lowered his head just as she raised hers, and he kissed her softly. When she kissed him back, Kenzo deepened the kiss, devouring her mouth, intermittingly sucking and teasing her tongue. Grace heard herself moan. She'd never been kissed like this. Never. Kenzo pulled her closer to him so she could feel his desire for her. Grace had never been so turned on from just a kiss. But this wasn't 'just' anything. This was delicious torture. She felt her nipples tighten, and her body felt like it was on fire. Grace couldn't remember how she ended up beneath Kenzo on the couch, but she didn't care once he started kissing, nibbling, and sucking her neck. She couldn't think past the pleasure of his mouth. Kenzo was cradling her to him with his right arm while his left hand was teasing her body.

Kenzo wanted to touch her, and when her legs parted of their own accord, he eased his hand toward her core. He felt the scrap of material between her legs, drenched with juices he felt a sudden urge to taste. Kenzo didn't know what was happening to his resolve, but he didn't care. He eased his fingers inside her, and she writhed beneath his ministrations. Her moans drove him to continue pleasuring her. It had been so long since Kenzo enjoyed the sounds of pleasure that he couldn't stop himself. He took the hand that had been holding her and brought it to her breast. He wanted to touch her everywhere at once. Kenzo felt like a drowning man given life.

Grace had never experienced such need, such pleasure. She knew this was too much too soon, she couldn't help herself from wanting him. It was as if her mouth and body knew his. She didn't want to think about how little they knew each other. She didn't want to think about whether this was appropriate. Grace just wanted to feel, and the way he was kissing and touching her, she was at pleasure overload. Her heartbeat was racing. His hands were magic. His fingers were making love to her all over, his kiss literally taking her breath away. She was helpless in his hands.

Kenzo knew she was close, and he never wanted anything so much at that moment. He wanted her to come apart in his hands. He couldn't explain it, but

Grace's pleasure was more important to him than his own. He stopped kissing her long enough to whisper, "Come for me, Grace."

It was electric, and Grace's body shattered. Kenzo felt her tighten around his fingers. Her moans were the sweetest music to his ears, and he kissed her deeply one final time before extracting his fingers from her core. Through half-closed eyes, Grace breathlessly whispered his name. Kenzo captured her mouth again, but he knew that if he didn't pull away, he was going to make love to her on this very spot.

———

Grace had been reading the same paragraph for twenty minutes. The article on immigrant trafficking as domestic labor just wasn't holding her interest. Grace hadn't been able to concentrate all day; she'd faked her way through her team meeting. She let Terry and Luther school the newbies about detective work while she sat back and listened. The team was learning about each other, and she was learning about them. But when they left the office suite, Grace was left alone with her memories of the night before. The memories were so fresh in her mind, that Grace was aroused again. They didn't make love, but both knew that they came awfully close. But Grace realized that even though they didn't, she would have been just fine if they had. Real fine. Grace shuddered at the thought of making love to Kenzo. He'd already shattered her once with his magic fingers, and if his kisses were any indication, she knew making love to him would be off the Richter scale.

"What are you thinking about, Grace."

Grace almost gave herself whiplash at the sound of that voice. Kenzo. She looked up, and there he was, leaning against her doorframe, looking sexy as hell. Caught and with no reason to lie, Grace looked him in the eye and said one word. "You."

CHAPTER 7

Zara walked into the restaurant scanned the room quickly. The cryptic note placed on her windshield said that her contact would be seated at a table in the back and near the window. No name. No description. She was going in blind. There were two single people seated at nearby tables, one male and one female, and she hoped that by the time she neared, she would be able to discern just who she was supposed to be meeting. A mistake at this juncture would be disastrous for this operation.

Zara walked determinedly toward the two tables. The man was smiling at her. Smiling politely, she noted that he was an African American male, well dressed, and very handsome. Extremely handsome. He definitely fit the profile. But the woman, a stunning older Indian woman dressed in an expensive black suit gave her a passing, disdainful glance and returned to her menu. She was about to approach the man when the Indian woman made a slight movement with her left hand. The Indian woman fingered her necklace, making the ring on her third finger visible, revealing herself as the connect. The ring matched the one she wore, a gold band adorned with precious jewels in the shape of a peacock.

She reached the woman's table, and without a word, she took a seat. The two women stared at each other for a moment. She was the one who had been summoned, so she waited, nervously rubbing her palms on her pants leg and watched the woman take another sip of her tea. This meeting was unexpected. And unexpected meant something was wrong.

"I hear the woman has taken you under her wing."

She nodded. "Yes, it's a small task force, so I've really gotten a chance to gain her trust and learn from her."

"I see. Good. Remember gain her trust. But never lose sight of your commitment." She paused, before adding, "And your loyalties." The woman's brow raised, and Zara took note of the veiled threat that wasn't so veiled.

"I haven't forgotten."

"We expect results. And that means we expect this woman and this crusade of hers to go away. And quickly. Understood?"

Zara nodded. "I know my responsibilities."

"Good. This is just a friendly visit, but make no mistake, it won't be friendly long if this Grace Harrington succeeds in any way. After this, we will continue to use the preferred communications. You will let us know something soon, yes?"

"Yes." Zara's cell phone started ringing, and she hesitated to answer it.

"Go on. Answer it. I hate those things."

She pulled her cell phone from her pocket, and rising from the table, answered the phone. "Zara Bailey." As she listened to the caller on the other line, the nameless Indian woman waved her away. Zara turned on her heel and walked out of the restaurant. In a different time and place, she would have never agreed to something like this, but her mother's medical bills and her father's gambling debts bankrupted the family. If she could sabotage the task force, they would erase her father's debt. She had no choice.

CHAPTER 8

The groundbreaking for the Noelle Project was scheduled in a month, and Kenzo was finalizing details for the festivities. He'd originally planned for a small gathering of family, friends, and early supporters of the project. But it ballooned into a bigger event than he'd ever planned, but he understood the politics. It was now a community event, with food and fireworks. He contacted retailers who already signed their leases and asked them to sponsor the event but to also send their hiring managers. A tent would be set up for applications and interviews. All retailers were contractually obligated that ten percent of the workforce be from Harrington Heights. That was non-negotiable.

He was reviewing the formal program when Riley burst into the room with a huge grin.

"So, I have to hear from Larry in the mailroom that you been catting around with Grace Harrington?"

Kenzo glanced at Riley, before returning to his computer screen. He didn't want to look at Riley. "What are you doing in the mailroom?"

"Stop trying to change the subject."

Kenzo chuckled. "Nothing to tell. We enjoy each other's company. That's all." Just thinking about Grace had him hard. They had been together every day for the last two weeks, but he hadn't taken her back to his house since then. Kenzo couldn't explain the deep, soul-stirring need for her, but he wasn't ready to take the next step. And he knew that the next time he took her to his home, she was going to be in his bed. She was breaking down every wall, every ounce of control he'd built in the last five years. But he was weakening fast. Kissing her wasn't enough anymore. He needed more, and he believed she wanted more as well.

"Hello? Are you listening to me?" Riley was thoroughly amused. "I knew this Harrington woman was trouble, but not like this. Damn, Kenzo, you've been out of the game a while. Every single woman in Jackson, hell in Mississippi, is ready to cut this girl. You turn them down for five years, and now you been spotted at restaurants, the movies, everywhere. You know what you're doing?"

"Yeah, man. I'll be honest. You know how devastated I was after Noelle died. And it wasn't just that she was gone, but that I wouldn't be able to make it all up to her. I just wasn't the husband she deserved." Kenzo sighed. "But I want to tell you. Grace is different from any woman I've ever known. She's smart. She's gorgeous. We just have a great time together."

Riley nodded his head. He was one of the few people who knew just how Kenzo punished himself. Celibacy for five years. Riley winced at the thought. He enjoyed the company of women on a regular basis. He was upfront about his expectations of a 'no strings attached' affair. If they started to get clingy, he moved on quickly. He had no plans of getting married, settling down, or any of that crap. Ever. "So is your sexual exile over?" Riley leaned forward in anticipation of his answer.

Kenzo shrugged. "No, not yet. We're just getting to know each other. I'm enjoying, what the old folks always called it, courting her like a gentleman. I have to get this right this time. If you ever had a date with any conversation, you'd understand."

With a raised eyebrow, Riley responded. "Very funny. I date intelligent women. We just don't talk. But, Kenzo, you sound like you're talking love and marriage?"

Kenzo stared at his friend and shook his head. "No, chivalry isn't dead, brother. And when it's over, we part as human beings. I don't need a woman vandalizing my car. How much was that paint job by the way?"

"Shit, man. Don't even bring that up." Changing the subject, Riley asked, "So, when do I get to meet her? I have to meet the woman who got you in the dating game again."

Kenzo laughed. "She'll be at the groundbreaking, so you can meet her then. But please, be on your best behavior."

RIley left his office to work on another deal. They were looking at a revitalization project downtown, and Riley took the lead on this one. Kenzo was glad. He trusted Riley completely, and he knew he'd bring him in when it was time.

Kenzo put down his pen and massaged his temples. Talking to Riley gave him a headache. What was happening to him? Since that night at his house, he hadn't trusted himself with her. Kenzo didn't want to rush, and frankly, it had been so long since he'd been with a woman, that he was unsure of himself. Kenzo and Grace had been together every day, and he'd enjoyed walking with her, talking with her, and just being in her presence.

Riley's question worried him. Was he falling in love again? And with Grace? He didn't know. With Noelle, he knew he loved her, but he was just too immature to fully appreciate the emotion of it all. And now, his emotions were all over the place, and in that moment, he needed to see Grace. And need was the word. It was 3:30 p.m., and even though they'd made a decision to wait until the end of the day at 5:00 p.m., he couldn't help himself. He accepted that Grace had become a part of him, quickly and absolutely.

He stood abruptly from his desk, telling Carolyn to lock up as he hurried to the elevator. Having their offices in the same building was a blessing and a curse, and today, it was a bit of both.

Grace was looking out of her office window, thinking about her team meeting. Something was off, but she couldn't put her finger on it. And that bothered her. Edward was really starting to get on her nerves. He was a wildcard. And wildcards could be a problem. She made a mental note to review his jacket and speak to him. She thought he could be a great asset, but he was working her nerves. He was still working Darknet trails and was getting some intel, but his attitude was hurting the dynamic of the group.

Grace's body knew the moment Kenzo entered her office. She turned away, and the sight of him made her take a step back. The cool of the window only highlighted the heat she felt. He walked slowly toward her, and Grace was held captive by the intensity of his look. She thought he looked as predatory as a panther stalking prey. She felt her panties dampen and her nipples harden against her blouse. She felt this need in her core that consumed her. Her heart was beating so hard and fast, she just knew he could hear it.

All Kenzo could see was Grace. Specifically, Grace's mouth. He needed to taste her, to feel her lips on his. He didn't care that he couldn't explain this all-consuming desire for her. He reached her and cupped her face in his hands and took her mouth. Grace gasped, and that's all the opening he needed to deepen the kiss. His tongue found hers, and he explored her mouth while his hands roamed her body. He couldn't tell her moans from his. In her passion, Grace was pulling his shirt out of his pants and wrapped her arms around him. Her hands on Kenzo's back felt like an electric shock, almost like she was branding him. He couldn't get enough of her taste on his tongue. He knew he was close to making love to her against that window, but that's not how he wanted his first time with Grace to be.

Reluctantly, Kenzo broke the kiss so they could breathe. Grace's arousal perfumed the air, and she was breathing hard. Neither of them could speak but he looked at her, and a calm washed over him.

He was in love with Grace Harrington.

He kissed her forehead and held her tighter. Grace found her voice and looked at him, trying to determine what brought that on.

"Kenzo, that was intense. Is anything wrong?"

Kenzo's brow furrowed slightly. He knew she didn't understand. "I just needed you. Can you leave now? I'm hungry. You?" Kenzo looked at her flushed face and kiss-swollen lips and knew that she was the most beautiful woman he'd ever seen.

Everything in Grace knew that he was deflecting. But she learned over the last couple of weeks that Kenzo was private but would open up freely when he was ready. Still relishing being in Kenzo's arms, Grace placed her head on his chest and let out a contented sigh. "Yes, after a kiss like that, I'm definitely hungry. Where to, Mr. Dallas?"

"Home. I'll order something. Any requests?"

"None. You've been full of surprises already, so just keep it going."

Kenzo gave her a sly grin. "Touché." With a quick kiss, he released her from his hold. "Meet me at the house in an hour?"

She nodded and watched him leave. She had just enough time to go home, change, and get to Kenzo's for dinner.

Dinner was wonderful. Kenzo didn't order but decided to cook for her. She chuckled. Men usually could make only a few dishes. Spaghetti and whatever meat could be grilled. She smiled at the sight of him standing over the stove. He'd changed into jeans and a black T-shirt that showcased the strength and tone of his biceps. The jeans hung low on his hips, and she could see how fit he was. Grace licked her lips. She'd never seen anything so sexy and virile in a man.

He asked her to stir while he made salad. As large as the kitchen is, she couldn't help but notice how many times they found ways to touch each other. It was a beautiful dance between them, as if they were in sync. When he "checked" on her stirring, she rolled her eyes at him, and he kissed the bridge of her nose. She couldn't imagine a more perfect evening. And she and Jaden never cooked together. He thought it was her job to cook and serve. The sight of Kenzo cutting and chopping ingredients for the salad was enough to make her fan herself.

Kenzo has never felt at home like he did right now. He felt an immediate sense of sadness that he hadn't done more of this for Noelle. He looked at Grace stirring the sauce, tasting and adding spices as she saw fit. She moved about the kitchen like she'd been there before, like it was hers. And Kenzo realized that he liked the idea of her feeling that way. He wanted her to feel at home here more than anything.

They continued their banter over dinner. At a lull in the conversation, Kenzo rose from the table, picking up both plates and heading for the kitchen. Grace followed him, methodically clearing the table. Neither spoke, but she felt the air change between them. Her body was humming in anticipation of what she'd hoped was coming. He hadn't brought her back here since that first real date, and she knew that the kiss they shared earlier was a preview of the passion and heat they would generate.

Kenzo reached out his hands for hers. In three measured steps forward, Grace placed her hands in his. Kenzo pulled her to him, cupped he face, and kissed her gently. "I want you, Grace. Let me make love to you tonight. If you think it's too soon, I'll understand. We can watch a movie or..."

Grace leaned her head back, placing her forefinger on his lips to stop him. "Make love to me, Kenzo," she whispered. "Make me yours."

Kenzo bent down, scooped her into his arms, and began walking to the bedroom. He cradled her to him, kissing her as he walked to the Master suite. Kenzo gently placed her on his king-sized bed and began undressing her. She'd worn a mint green pullover that complemented her skin beautifully. He dispatched that quickly, and almost groaned out loud when he saw the lacy black bra she wore and her nipples straining against it. "You are so beautiful, Grace," he whispered. "So damn beautiful." He undid the front clasp, and as her breasts sprang free, he caressed both and teased her nipples as she squeezed her legs together.

Kenzo found the waistband of her khaki skirt she wore and unbuttoned it. Grace lifted her hips as he pulled the skirt down, revealing a matching pair of black lace panties. Kenzo inhaled. He would never forget her scent as long as he lived. Removing her panties was the most difficult. He wanted to take it slow, but the sight of her naked and in his bed brought out something primal in him. He had to control his base instinct to mount her and begin thrusting forward.

He stood at the foot of the bed to undress, his eyes never leaving hers. She was a vision before him, one already seared into his memory. Grace looked as if she belonged there, in his bed, waiting for him to deliver promised pleasures. There were no promises, but after tonight there would be.

Grace heard her heart beating in her ears and could swear she could feel the blood rushing through her veins. If looking at him was having this effect, she didn't know how she was going to survive his touch. Kenzo was standing at the foot of the bed, looking so sexy, so unbelievably male, that Grace was spellbound. He was staring at her so intensely and was standing so still that he resembled a statue. All of him. The intensity of his desire-filled gaze took her breathe away.

Grace's eyes slowly raked the full length of him, counting each chiseled muscle and then tracing the "v" to his full erection. The gasp escaped her mouth before she could stop it, and she felt the flush of wetness between her legs. Embarrassed, she forced her eyes to meet his again but there was no mirth in his eyes, only a determination that, quite frankly, scared her. She wasn't that sexually experienced, but no experience could have prepared her for the sensuality of that act. Not to mention that he protected her automatically and without any prodding.

Kenzo watched her as he rolled on a condom, her eyes getting even wider.

Just her looking at him was making it difficult to breathe, but he knew he had to summon some semblance of control. He'd always worn a condom before he married, but he'd been celibate since Noelle's death. Luckily, the market hadn't changed much. Kenzo shook his head to clear his thoughts. Right now, he didn't want to think about anything but the woman in front of him. His Grace. He could only imagine what loving her with no barrier would feel like. He almost lost all control at the thought.

Kenzo watched her appreciate his body as he appreciated hers. The gold-flecked nail polish on her toes seem to dance with the light and the white sheet highlighted her bronze complexion. Suddenly, he was overwhelmed with desire and a need to taste her. He moved forward, and he saw what looked like fear flash across her face. Was she really that afraid of him? No. He knew she wanted him, but just to be sure, he thought he would start slowly. He took in a deep breath, trying to control himself. If he gave in to his desires the way he wanted, she would be scared...at first. He placed a knee on the bed, holding her gaze, lifting her left foot to massage it. He felt her body relax as he continued his ministrations. As her eyelids lowered, he placed soft kisses on her instep. Her soft moans motivated him but made it harder to gain his control. He drew her hallux into his mouth, and she started squirming.

"Don't move," he said huskily as he looked at her hard. "I want you to feel all of what I'm going to do to you." He nibbled on each toe as she made a feeble attempt to comply with his demands.

Grace thought she was going to pass out. How could she not move? Was he insane? She had never had anyone do that. Lord, have mercy. She was so glad she splurged on the pedicure. She threw her head back on the pillow and exhaled, willing herself still lest he stop again.

He tasted her smooth skin and inhaled the vanilla scent from the body wash she used. After kissing and laving attention on her feet, he crawled up the length of her body, kissing and licking the inside of her legs. He could feel the tremors of her legs as he watched her clutch the sheet to gain control. He smiled against the bend in her knee. Grace felt like every nerve in her body was on fire as he moved up the length of her, kissing, sucking, nibbling as if she were a delicious meal.

He could smell her arousal, which heightened his own. He didn't know how he was going to survive it. Her scent was driving him mad and he reminded himself that this was for her. His Grace. Summoning control, he nudged her legs open a bit more and took one long leisurely lick up her right inner thigh and sucked and nibbled her trembling flesh from the top of her inner thigh to her knee. He repeated the motion on the left and her moans almost took him over the edge. He nestled himself squarely at her mound, watching her womanly core contract in anticipation. He suddenly changed course and decided to wait. She was ready, but he wasn't.

Kenzo could see her hardened nipples rise and fall with each labored breath. Overwhelmed with the sudden urge to kiss her, he positioned himself about her and as soon as he did so, her eyes opened, tears threatening to fall. He bent his head and gently nudged her head to the side to give him access to her throat. He assaulted her throat, marking her at the jugular as his woman. And she was his. His Grace.

Even if she didn't know it yet.

Not remotely satisfied, he tasted her mouth, kissing her deeply, pouring everything he'd ever wanted for her and them in it. She was his grace.

When he broke the kiss, they were both breathless. But he wasn't done pleasuring her. He could feel her nipples against his chest and the friction was driving him insane. He slid down her body; her scent was growing stronger in his nostrils, but he hadn't tasted her breasts. He placed feather-soft kisses at the swell of each perfect breast before licking the underside of each, finally taking a nipple in his mouth. He manipulated one nipple between his fingers while sucking the other. His control was waning, but she deserved more control than his natural instincts to plunder would allow. He kissed, sucked, and caressed her breasts until they were both on the verge of madness. After giving each ample and equal attention, Kenzo shifted, nestling himself, again, between her legs and inhaled her scent. As soon as he placed his tongue on her clit, she screamed.

He held her legs still as she came, forcing her body to absorb the pleasure. Just as her first orgasm waned, he tortured them both further, driving her toward another as he darted his tongue in and out of her in the same rhythm as his manhood would make in a few moments. When Grace's second orgasm hit, he felt the pulse of it in his groin.

He sheathed her quickly and entered her on a hard thrust. He stopped to give her time to adjust to him and to give himself time to regain control. She was his, and she felt so good. And, tonight, he wanted her body to know it at a cellular level. He whispered in her ear with each thrust. "I love you, Grace. Only you."

Between each whisper he kissed away the tears that had fallen. She began moving against him and soon, their rhythm was as one. She met him stroke for stroke, and Kenzo knew they were both close.

Kenzo could no longer hold back, her moans and whimpers took his senses. "Come with me, baby. Come with me, Grace."

Grace exploded around him, screaming his name. Surely, she'd be hoarse once this night was over. The contractions from her orgasms set off his, and their voices rent the air. Kenzo couldn't hold back the primal yell at his release. He'd never come so hard in his life. He had never been pushed to the limit of control. He'd never felt so utterly complete in his passion for another woman. For the first time in his life, he felt complete.

As their orgasms subsided, Kenzo kissed her deeply, reluctantly leaving her warmth. They both winced at the separation. Grace's eyes were still closed, her breathing still ragged but calming. He propped himself on his side, pulling her closer to him. He desperately needed the contact, and he felt himself wanting her again. But first, he needed to know how she was feeling. He hoped she didn't have any regrets about being with him. Though her breathing slowed to normal, she still hadn't opened her eyes.

Grace felt Kenzo's gaze, but she didn't want to open her eyes. She would have to face reality. She was in love with Kenzo, and she didn't know if he were really in love with her, or if he just said it in the heat of the moment. His touch was torture. She could feel his intensity, and was he already ready again? Impossible. No. Not with Kenzo. It was absolutely possible.

Kenzo whispered, "Grace. Open your eyes, baby. Talk to me."

Grace's eyelids fluttered opened, and Kenzo let out a breath he didn't know he was holding.

"Are you okay? Tell me what you're thinking. No, tell me what you're feeling."

Grace looked at the chiseled features of Kenzo's face and then forced herself to look into those hazel eyes that had captured her heart from the moment she saw them. She opened her mouth to speak and closed it. She had no words for him.

Kenzo searched her face. She was so beautiful. Her hair tousled; her lips swollen from his kisses. The curve of her breast rising and falling with each breath. But it was always her huge, brown eyes that he drowned in each and every time he looked at her.

"Grace. I need you to talk to me."

Grace heard the anguish, the pleading in his voice.

Grace said softly, "Oh, Kenzo. I have never..." Her voice caught in her throat. Kenzo rubbed her arms to soothe her as she summoned the courage to speak. "No one has ever loved me like that before. That was...you touched my soul, Kenzo."

He closed his eyes to keep his own tears from falling. "Grace," he whispered, "you are my world, and I never want you to think or feel otherwise. Everything I am and have is yours. My heart. My soul." Kenzo lowered his head to kiss her gently, but with every ounce of the love he had for her in the kiss, the kiss became more powerful, igniting his desire again. Grace returned his kiss just as passionately, and they made love again and again until morning.

CHAPTER 9

Kenzo Dallas spared no expense when it came to the groundbreaking ceremony and reception for the Noelle Project, now officially named the Dallas Harrington Shopping Center. Thankfully, it was a beautiful Mississippi day, warm but not blistering heat, and even a few gentle breezes. Every time the wind caressed his face, Kenzo felt as though Noelle was there. As the mayor made his remarks, a breeze touched his face. Kenzo closed his eyes, silently praying that God and Noelle were pleased. When he opened his eyes, they landed on the beautiful woman he'd fallen in love with, the one who unthawed his heart, Grace Harrington. She'd taken a seat in one of the seats in the back of the audience, and Kenzo appreciated the discreet gesture. Grace understood how important this day was for him, and she'd even helped with the final detailing for the reception. By now, people surmised that they were dating, but this wasn't the time for that. He gave her an acknowledging smile before returning his attention to the mayor, who was wrapping up his remarks about how important the shopping center was to the uplift of the area. Kenzo was impressed with the young mayor; he'd brought a great deal of vitality to Jackson and seemed truly connected to the community. And he'd been on board from the beginning, which meant a lot to Kenzo when he needed as much support as he could get.

After the mayor, his former mother-in-law spoke. Mrs. Teresa Jonesboro stood proudly at the podium, wearing her daughter's last gift to her, a white suit with gold appliqué. Her smooth caramel skin and high cheekbones reflected her African American and Cherokee heritage. She stood proud, and Kenzo imagined Noelle at that age standing just as proud as her mom. Mrs. Jonesboro spoke to the audience about Noelle's innocence and giving spirit as a child, laughing as she told the story about Noelle putting in all of her money in the collection plate for all her friends. Even though Kenzo had heard the story countless times, he chuckled as if it had been the first time. Kenzo realized how good it felt to laugh and celebrate Noelle rather than wallow in mourning as he had.

When the laughter faded and emotion overtook Teresa, Kenzo's mother, in her white ceremonial Yoruba robe and gele, stood with her for support. Kenzo looked at the two women who held him up when Noelle died. They were proud women who had endured much and mourned together. Noelle was as much a daughter to Mbetha Dallas as if she'd birthed her. Noelle's death hit his mother, and his father for that matter, just as hard. And yet, both women gave him everything they could to help him through his mourning.

As Ms. Jonesboro talked, Kenzo thought about how unnatural it all was. No mother should have to bury her child. Though she was skeptical at first, Teresa and Kenzo forged an incredible bond in the last five years. Their shared loss made it so. She had been the only person to whom he'd been able to confess his sins, and her forgiveness gave him the strength to make a life for himself. And when he'd told her about Grace, she'd been happy for him and they cried together. Kenzo teared up at the memory of being held by his late wife's mother while he cried over falling in love with someone else.

Then, it was his turn to speak. Getting himself together, Kenzo walked slowly to the podium. He hugged and kissed his mother and mother-in-law and led them to their seats. Once there, he took a cleansing breath. His exhale was audible in the sensitive microphone. He surveyed the audience. All of Noelle's friends were there, even the ones who had never really cared for him. He invited them hoping that they loved her more than they ever hated him. And they had. Riley gave him a supportive nod, encouraging him to begin. He looked up at the sky, the breeze had returned. When he brought his head down, Grace was standing directly in his sight line, and the calm of the breeze and the sight of Grace, gave him the strength to speak.

"Ladies and Gentlemen, to my wife and me, Jackson was and will always be home. All of it. And Harrington Heights always held a special place in her heart. She went to church around the corner on Ridgeway. She travelled these streets to work, to school, and in life. And where most of us saw poverty and blight, she saw opportunity and promise. I dismissed her notions so many times. But when she died, the only way I could honor her was to make Jackson and Harrington Heights into the place she envisioned. And I hope that I..." Kenzo stopped. He wasn't expecting the rush of emotion that seized him in that moment.

"I hope that her spirit is proud of the work we've done as a community and a city." Kenzo felt the breeze caress his cheek. "I know that Noelle's spirit is here, and I hope she is proud."

Grace stood still. She watched the man who had become so important to her speak so lovingly about the project and his deceased wife. During the last few weeks, Kenzo and Grace had been inseparable when they weren't working in their respective offices. She was drawn to the passion in his words, and she completely understood that protecting and respecting Noelle's memory would always be important to him. Grace, surprisingly, realized that the project was important to her as well, because it was important to him.

Grace watched Kenzo leave the platform. Everyone was headed to the site where the first shovel would be pitched into the earth. Kenzo ordered commemorative construction hats for everyone invited, and she donned hers as she made her way to the designated area. Everyone was given a white tulip, Noelle's favorite flower, to lay on the mound in her memory. At first, she thought it would be depressing, like they were having a second funeral, but after the emotion and significance of the day, she admitted that Kenzo had the right idea. Kenzo informed her that Noelle loved white tulips because they symbolized forgiveness, and everyone at some point in their lives needed to ask for, be granted, and grant forgiveness.

Grace watched Kenzo and Riley take the commemorative shovels in hand. Kenzo, of course, was the first to pierce the dirt, followed by Riley. Mrs. Jonesboro even dipped her shovel in, visibly moved by the moment. The tulips that lay across the upturned earth made a serene sight, and as people walked back toward their cars to leave, she heard them all reminisce about Noelle and remarking on how lovely the day was.

As she waited for Kenzo at his car, she felt her senses go on alert. The air changed around her, Grace got the eerie sense that she was being watched. She looked around, and her hand automatically went to her hip for her gun. She silently cursed when she realized that not only did she not have her firearm, but also that she automatically went for it. *Get a grip, Grace,* she said to herself. Still, she thought it best to scan the dissipating crowd. She'd met most of the attendees before the ceremony, so she focused on the faces that weren't readily identifiable. There was one figure whose face was obstructed from her view, but just as she decided to get closer, she saw Kenzo walking directly toward her. He looked emotionally spent despite the beautiful smile on his face. Grace couldn't smiled back at him. He was gorgeous in a white linen suit that highlighted his bronze skin. *Damn, he was sex walking*, she thought. Grace shook her head, admonishing herself for such thoughts at a time such as this. But he looked so good she couldn't help it. At the sight of him, she completely forgot that she was supposed to be looking for someone. She only saw Kenzo.

Kenzo's arms opened for her, and she walked straight into them. He kissed the top of her head and held her for a moment. Kenzo's emotions were still raw from the ceremony, and he needed this moment with Grace to steady himself. Grace said nothing, and as strong as he was, Kenzo knew that she was holding him up at that moment. He released her and immediately felt the loss of contact. He opened the passenger side door without a word, and she slid onto the seat. Kenzo walked to his side of the car. He looked back at the site and mass of tulips before opening his door and getting in.

"Tired?" Kenzo looked over at Grace, who was stunning in a white sundress with yellow flowers.

"A little, but I'll manage. Kenzo, the ceremony was beautiful, and Noelle's mother just took my breath away. I can't imagine the pain she feels every day."

"I know. She has been a blessing in this whole plan. I really couldn't have done it without her."

They fell into a comfortable silence as Kenzo drove Grace back to her grandmother's house to prepare for the formal reception that evening. The reception would be at the University Club, and Grace would be meeting most of his family and friends. This wasn't exactly the way she'd ever want to meet her man's people. Kenzo invited Treasure, but she was out of town on a shopping trip and didn't know if she would have returned in time. Grace silently prayed that her friend could find an earlier flight. Grace felt petty, but she wanted her friend there for support. She thought about not going. After all, this was to honor Noelle, and she didn't want her presence to be a distraction, or worse, regarded as inappropriate. This was still the South, and still Mississippi. Proper still mattered here if nowhere else in the world.

It was as if Kenzo could read her mind. "Please don't back out on me tonight. I know this is a lot, but it will mean the world to me to have you by my side tonight." His hands were gripping the steering wheel tightly. Grace could see the strain in his features, and his knuckles were almost white.

"I just don't want to be a distraction tonight. I'm the first woman you've dated since Noelle's death. I'm worried about the optics of you bringing a date to a reception honoring your late wife."

"I thought about that, Grace. I did." Kenzo took his right hand off the wheel and reached for hers. She felt his warmth as their fingers clasped. Grace shivered. It was like he could warm her entire body with a touch. "Just knowing you're there will help me get through this night."

Grace looked at their hands, and over at Kenzo. "I'll be there. And we'll get through it together."

Grace selected a sleek black gown for the reception. She wanted to look nice and conservative and blend into the wall if necessary. This really wasn't the way she wanted to be introduced, but Kenzo insisted that he needed her. And she knew that was a lot for him to admit to her. *Lord, please let this night go well.* Kenzo was to pick her up at 6:30 since he wanted to be there early to make sure everything was set up properly. She took a quick nap, packed an overnight bag, showered, dressed, and applied her make-up with fifteen minutes to spare. She was giving herself one last look in the mirror when the doorbell rang.

She picked up her purse from the hall table, opened the door, and almost passed out. It wasn't Kenzo, but Jaden. *You have got to be kidding me,* Grace thought. She blinked a couple of times to see if she was seeing things.

But she wasn't.

Jaden was standing on her grandmother's porch bold as hell, standing there with his trademark, disingenuous smile. He was giving her the smile he gave when he was running game and up to no earthly good. It was one she knew all too well. Even worse, he could tell she was taken by surprise.

Grace offered a dry greeting, hoping that her displeasure at the sight of him was clearly obvious. "Hello, Jaden. Why are you here, and when are you leaving?" She wanted him gone before Kenzo pulled up. That's the last thing she needed or wanted. Tonight, especially.

Jaden seemed taken aback by her attitude. His smile faded and he traded it for his equally disgusting trademark attitude. "Aren't you happy to see me, baby? It's been a while. Let me in, Grace."

"Clearly, not long enough. And no, I will not let you in. I'm leaving for an event shortly, and my date will be here in a moment. I want you gone before he gets here. You and I have nothing to say to each other." She was grateful that her grandmother was at church for her mission meeting. Otherwise, she would have been forced to allow him in.

"Date? Some country bama?" He laughed out loud, and Grace wanted to smack him, but that would require touching him, so she couldn't do that. Jaden saw that Grace was getting angry, so he switched his approach. Somberly, he said, "But I want to give us another chance. Surely, by now, you've had a chance to calm down."

"Calm down?" Grace was incredulous. She couldn't believe that she considered marrying this man. At one point, she thought she actually loved him. *Please, Lord, forgive me. The nerve of him.* Grace continued to block his entry. He knew not to attempt to push his way inside. Through clenched teeth, Grace said, "I told you to leave. And do not come here again. Remember, when I told you we have Castle Law in Mississippi and how I thought it was awful? Well, I've just changed my mind. I'm still a better shot than you." For emphasis, she added, "And you know I don't miss." Grace walked forward and closed the door behind her, forcing him to back up.

As soon as she closed the door, Grace heard Kenzo's car approaching but continued to stare at Jaden. He was trying to return her stare, but when the car came to a full stop, he turned and saw Kenzo's Mercedes. The look on his face was priceless. Grace laughed, "What? You thought I was going to a hayride in a pickup truck?"

Grace looked past Jaden and saw that Kenzo had exited the car and was coming toward the porch. Kenzo looked sexy as hell in his Armani tuxedo, and she couldn't help but smile at him. She could tell he was trying to assess the situation and figure out who Jaden was. Before he asked, Grace decided to take the initiative and clear up several items. "Hey, baby," she purred, "I'm ready." She wanted Jaden to know that this man coming to her was more than a date.

Kenzo assessed the brother standing there and looked at Grace. Grace looked beautiful as always, but he could tell something was off with her. Her mouth was saying one thing, but he'd come to know her body well enough to know when she was nervous, scared, frustrated, and above all, angry. But this was apprehension. Kenzo decided to play along until he got the answers he wanted.

"Hey, Love. Who's your friend?" He kept his eyes on Grace as he walked up the porch steps. He could tell the man was trying to determine several things about the nature of his relationship with Grace, but he wasn't ready to acknowledge him just yet. When he reached the porch, he held his arms open and Grace walked into them. He planted a sweet kiss on her forehead. "You, okay?"

Grace heard the edge in Kenzo's voice, and she knew that Jaden heard it. "I'm fine. Kenzo, this is my ex-fiancé, Jaden Burke." Kenzo released her, but held her hand, keeping her close to him. He rubbed the back of her hand with his thumb, which calmed her nerves. Grace wondered how he always knew what to do to make her feel safe.

Kenzo glanced at Jaden. He extended his right hand to Jaden. "Kenzo Dallas. What do we owe the pleasure?" Grace wanted to laugh out loud, but she was enjoying watching the show. She was enjoying watching Kenzo work. Kenzo made it clear that there was a "we," and Grace felt her heart expand.

Jaden stammered his response. "I was in the area and thought I'd stop by, but I see you have plans. I guess I should have called." He tried to end on a laugh, but it fell flat.

"Yes, Grace and I do have plans," and turning to Grace, "we better get going, Sweetheart." Kenzo offered his hand again to Jaden, "Good to meet you man, and thank you. Thank you very much." Without another word, Kenzo led Grace to the passenger side of the door and opened it for her. As Grace slid into the seat, Kenzo looked at her and gave her a soft nod. He rounded the car and got inside, revved the engine, and drove away.

Jaden was left standing on the porch, embarrassed and seething.

Kenzo and Grace made a silent pact not to discuss Jaden's appearance on her doorstep. Kenzo looked at Grace, who had fallen into a tense silence, and he could feel her tension ripple through her. He opened his hand for hers, and Grace, saying nothing, placed her hand in his. Grace kept her eyes focused on the road ahead, but Kenzo felt her relax. Kenzo was hoping that the evening would be a pleasurable one. Despite the emotion of the day, Kenzo surprised himself by being so relaxed.

When he dropped Grace off after the morning's ceremony, he went to Noelle's grave. Though he knew that he'd felt her presence at the ceremony, he needed this time with Noelle alone. He sat on the hard earth and pulled the weeds that had grown around her tombstone, speaking to the cold marble as if she could and would respond. As he always did, he apologized for hurting her and thanked her for loving and caring for him the way she did. Kenzo told her about the day, how her mother told the collection plate story, how beautiful the ceremony was, and how Harrington Heights would become the place she'd always dreamed. He stood up and faced her tombstone and took a cleansing breath, wiping his hands down his face, and told her about Grace and how much she meant to him and that he loved her. Though it might not have made any sense to anyone, Kenzo needed Noelle's blessing. After a few moments, a gentle breeze caressed him, and he knew it was time to let go.

Even with the Jaden holdup, they'd made it at least thirty minutes before the reception would begin. Kenzo and Grace were on the elevator headed to the University Club. In these few moments before the chaos of the event, Kenzo needed some alone time with Grace as well. He released his first love today, and right now, he needed to embrace his new love. Kenzo pulled Grace to him, so she could feel how much he wanted her, even now. "Thank you for coming tonight," he whispered in her ear. He felt her shudder against him, and his thoughts took a salacious turn. Grace raised her eyes to his, and hoarsely whispered, "No need to thank me." Kenzo held her chin in place and kissed her softly.

"Have I told you how beautiful you look tonight?" Kenzo thought she was the most beautiful woman he'd ever seen, even more than that first night he'd seen her and didn't even know her name. "You're even more beautiful than the first time I saw you." He saw tears glistening in her eyes, and he kissed her again. He took advantage of her partly open mouth to deepen the kiss, and Grace could only grab the lapels of Kenzo's tuxedo. Their tongues danced until the ping of the elevator announced their arrival on the floor. Any other time, Kenzo would have stopped the elevator and taken her right there, but there would be more time for that later. He would make sure of it.

Grace's attempts to blend into the background were thwarted the moment the people started arriving. While she was perfectly content to mingle with a few people and move about stealthily and prayerfully unnoticed, Kenzo wouldn't hear of it. His and Noelle's parents were some of the first to arrive and they were together. It was in that moment that Grace realized just how close the families were and was at a loss on the protocols. Suddenly, Grace felt her heart constrict and start beating fast. Kenzo placed his hand at the small of her back as they walked toward them, and Grace felt his warmth flow throughout her. But as Kenzo kissed his mother and Ms. Jonesboro and began the introductions to her parents and former mother-in-law, the anxiety resurfaced. Both mothers were extremely gorgeous and took her breath away. Kenzo's mother looked like an African queen with her smooth ebony skin, reminding Grace of Cicely Tyson. Her African-inspired gown showed her shapely figure and was adorned with intricate beading. Grace didn't doubt that it was tailor made for her. Noelle's mother, wore a beautiful deep purple floor-length that complemented her warm café au lait color. She reminded Grace of her own mother—conservative, classy, and with a hint of mischief. Kenzo's father's was an extremely handsome, older version of Kenzo, and she could tell that he was still very much in love with Mbetha. Grace couldn't place his coloring in her mind but it was distinct; she could see how well his Asian and African American features blended. Grace extended her hand for the handshake and was taken aback when Mbetha pulled her in an embrace.

"Oh, no, dear, we are huggers around here. Kenzo's told me a lot about you. Are you enjoying being back home?"

"Yes, ma'am." Grace nodded, "it's been a true blessing to be home again, and hopefully make a difference in Jackson."

"I know your grandmother, Hettie. She's in my literary club. A spitfire, that one!" Mbetha laughed. "She's so proud of you, and I know she's glad you're back as well."

Grace laughed. "Yes, ma'am."

Grace didn't know what to do when Teresa Jonesboro broke in not to be outdone. "We all know Hettie and Mose, child. And your uncle and I were high school classmates."

After a little small talk, Grace felt at ease enough to lead them to their reserved table. Kenzo wanted to check on something with the band, so she was left alone with the elders. Grace excused herself to greet others, but not before Teresa grabbed her hand to get her attention. She hugged her tightly and whispered in Grace's ear. "Thank you. You've brought our boy back to us." She released her, and there were tears shining in both women's eyes. Grace could only nod at her, and after a moment, she walked away wiping away the tears that had fallen.

Though he was talking to other guests, Kenzo never let Grace out of his sight. He watched Grace interact with his parents and Teresa. He was thankful that his mother and Teresa embraced her as they had. Though he'd told them about her, he admitted that having them finally meet, on this night, in particular, wasn't ideal. It just couldn't be helped. He watched Grace walk away from their table and excused himself from the Mayor and his wife. It looked as if Grace was crying.

Grace stopped the moment Kenzo looked at her. She patted her face so he wouldn't see her tears and smiled at him.

"You're crying. Why?" Kenzo's voice was full of so much concern that more tears threatened to fall.

"Nothing. Your parents and Mrs. Jonesboro are so nice that I was just a little overwhelmed. I guess I didn't know what to expect." When he didn't look convinced, she reassured him. "Kenzo, I'm fine. Really, I am. I'd tell you if I wasn't."

Kenzo knew that she would. Taking her hand, he pulled her close to him. He needed the connection with her if only for a moment. And it was just a moment, because there was a commotion at the entrance. Kenzo recognized the man as Riley, he but didn't recognize the woman he was with. Kenzo heard Grace say, "Oh, hell..." and leave him for the couple. He followed close behind, trying to figure out just what trouble Riley had gotten himself into now.

Riley was furious, and despite not wanting to make a scene, he knew their escalated voices turned more than a few heads. "Listen, woman, I was trying to be a gentleman. Most women," he paused, "most sane women would appreciate my chivalry. But no, not you." Treasure Jordan was the only woman who could make him angry enough to spit nails and who could arouse him to distraction. Even now, he couldn't help but look at the curve of her breasts that were threatening to spill out of her dress, or the way her full lips moved even as she was yelling at him. Finally, he tore his eyes from her breasts, and looked into the angriest, most beautiful hazel eyes he'd ever seen. She was still as gorgeous as the first time he'd laid eyes on her three years ago.

"I don't need you to do a damn thing for me, Riley Taylor." Treasure was speaking to him through clenched teeth. "And you know why." Treasure couldn't believe her luck. Her best friend was falling in love with a man who was best friends with the most infuriating man she'd ever met. They had one disastrous date three years ago that ended in the best sex of her life. It was supposed to be a fling, and it was. One weekend. No attachments. And when the weekend ended, so did they. The ground rules were set, but part of her wished that they had broken them. She wanted to break them. But he obviously hadn't wanted to, or he would have called. All she got was a bouquet of flowers and a card that he'd probably sent to countless women. She was sure of that. *Thank you for a lovely time. Riley.* Just looking at him, now, made her blood boil. Treasure realized that Kenzo and Grace were on their way over and she needed to compose herself.

"Look, Kenzo and Grace are coming this way. She doesn't know anything, and I don't want her to know." For once, Riley agreed with her. He'd never told Kenzo about her either. He decided to throw her a bone. "Fine, I'll follow your lead." Treasure glared at him with the sexiest pout Rlley thought he'd ever seen.

Damn him, Treasure thought. Just as Kenzo and Grace reached them, Treasure plastered a smile on her face and thought she'd come up with a plausible story. Grace would be difficult. She was trained in detecting bullshit. Treasure decided to go on the offensive and steer the awkwardness in another direction. As soon as Grace was in arm's reach, she grabbed her.

"Girl, you look gorgeous! Where did you get that dress?" Treasure was playing it to the hilt, but soon realized that Grace wasn't buying what she was selling.

Grace's lips were set hard. "Treasure, you know very well where I got this dress. Your shop. Now, tell me what is going on?" The two friends stared at each other for a moment while Kenzo and Riley watched. Grace knew her friend. Something was wrong, and she was determined to find out what this was.

"Treasure, come with me to the restroom, please. I'm having an issue with my dress." Both women knew that was a gracious lie, giving them an exit and leaving Treasure's dignity intact. At least, Grace hoped that it would. Treasure nodded, leaving with one final glare at Riley.

Kenzo and Rlley watched the ladies walk toward the restrooms without a word to each other. When the ladies were safely out of earshot, Kenzo shook his head and chuckled.

"Man, I don't even want to know. But I'm sure you should tell me."

"Whatever, man. Point me in the direction of the bar."

CHAPTER 10

For once in his life, or at least in the last five years, Kenzo felt like living. Once the party was in full swing, Kenzo danced, and it felt good. He danced with his mother, Noelle's mother, twirling them around the dance floor like they were teenagers. But when Kenzo took Grace to the dance floor, he could tell she was impressed.

"Where did you learn to dance like that?" Grace was breathless. She'd never been effortlessly twirled and dipped. She noticed that Kenzo seemed lighter, happier, and his smile brighter. She knew that the weight of the last five years had been slowly wearing him down.

Kenzo looked sheepish and slightly embarrassed. "Mbetha was a formidable parent. We had to take dance classes, music lessons, play sports, and anything else she wanted us to do. I drew the line at ballet or anything with tights."

He twirled her again and brought her into his body. Without a word spoken between them, Grace felt his desire for her. Grace shivered when he pressed his hand possessively in the small of her back. Even through her dress, she felt a warmth she'd never experienced with any man. She looked into his eyes and wondered how she could have fallen so quickly, so completely for Kenzo, but she had.

In her best southern belle voice, "Why, Mr. Dallas, are you trying to tempt and tease me into being naughty this evening?"

Kenzo stopped short and pulled Grace in close enough for her feel his throbbing erection. He bent down and whispered huskily in her ear, "Make no mistake,

Ms. Harrington, I'm planning to use all of my powers of seduction tonight. And that is no tease."

Grace took in a sharp intake of breath. She felt his desire, thinking that it was impossible for him to have gotten bigger since the last time they'd made love. Just the thought of him had her body keyed up and in a frenzied wanting. Grace didn't recognize the yearning in her voice. "When do we leave?"

As soon as they entered Kenzo's home, Grace felt both of them exhale. The day had been an exhausting but fulfilling one, but she was still concerned that he hadn't mentioned Jaden being on her doorstep at all. It was if it all didn't happen. She watched him slip off his jacket throw it on the back of the sofa, pick up the remote, and turn on the stereo. The sounds of John Coltrane's saxophone filled the house. She had never been a jazz fan before, but Kenzo was enlightening her on its healing properties. She smiled. The genre was growing on her, like the man who introduced it to her.

As if he could sense her watching him, Kenzo turned toward her and extended his hand. "Come here," Kenzo said, so softly that she almost missed it. The intensity in his eyes heated her entire being, and Grace felt like she was floating toward him. She could only see his eyes, those gorgeous eyes and long lashes that any woman would kill to have, staring at her. Grace had never felt so wanted.

When she reached him, in one swift movement, he pulled her to him gently and kissed her sweetly yet hungrily. Between kisses, Kenzo whispered, "thank you for today." He'd overtaken her mouth and senses so that Grace could only respond by returning the fervor of his kiss. When Kenzo broke the kiss, he smiled at her. "I needed that, baby."

Grace nodded, adding, "I know today was hard for you, but it was so beautiful. You should be proud." Kenzo didn't respond but looked away, fighting the emotion bubbling inside him.

Changing the subject, "I need a good soak. Join me." It was part request, part demand, but Grace didn't care. Kenzo took her hand in his and led her to the master bedroom without another word. Despite the lightness of spirit that she felt at the reception, Grace could feel the tension rolling off him.

"Wait here." Kenzo ordered her to stand by the bed. Normally, she would have taken umbrage with the command, but Kenzo's command had no machismo in it. More like sad resignation. So, she waited.

Kenzo felt every muscle in his body coiled tight. Grace was right, it had been a beautiful day. And even his trip to the cemetery had been beautiful. During the reception, he'd been as happy as he'd ever remembered being, because he'd done this wonderful thing for his wife. His deceased wife. But now...now the reality had set in that it was done. He shook his head. *Talk about anticlimactic,* he thought to himself.

Kenzo turned the water on and adjusted the temperature. He lit the candles surrounding the tub and the fragrance of vanilla and jasmine was intensified by the steam. As the water ran, he went back into the bedroom. Grace was still standing in the same spot, devastatingly beautiful. The worried expression on her face made him love and want her more than he ever had.

"Kenzo?" Grace's eyes were questioning and worried.

He cupped her face and kissed her softly. Her dress had a side zipper, and without taking his eyes off hers, he unzipped her dress and let it pool at her feet. Kenzo placed his hands at her waist and hooked his thumbs in the waistband of her barely-there thongs. As he pulled them down, he could smell her arousal.

"Step."

Grace placed her hands on his shoulders to balance herself as she stepped out of her panties and shoes. Kenzo kissed her left calf before rising to lead her to the bath. Grace was glad she was still holding on for support, or she would have fallen from the sensuousness of the act. She was so turned on that she knew he could smell her essence because she could.

Kenzo helped her into the bath and turned on the whirlpool jets. Grace slid into the bath and eased toward the side to give him room. She watched him remove his clothing and she gasped at the sheer beauty of his physique. Not even fully erect, he was still impressive, and Grace wanted him.

Kenzo lowered himself into the whirlpool and let the water cover him. He opened his legs and motioned for Grace to come sit in front of him. When she leaned back into his body, Kenzo felt a stirring in his groin, but he really wanted to just hold her for a moment. Grace leaned her head back and waited for him to speak. He lathered the towel with soap and nudged her forward. He washed her back, almost mesmerized by the interplay of the soap and water dancing down her back as he cleansed and massaged her. He kissed the top of her spine as the last of the water washed away the suds. Her moans of pleasure increased his own desire.

Finished with her back, Kenzo lathered up the towel again. He placed the soapy towel on her shoulder and let the soap run over her shoulder. He closed his eyes, imagining the lather trickling around and down her breasts. He reached around her to cup her breasts, washing one while massaging the other. He teased her nipples with his hands and the towel, kissing the sweet spot at that base of her ear. He shifted focus as he moved the towel between her legs, gently bathing her most intimate areas and grazing the sensitive bud that was swollen with desire.

Grace was nearly delirious from Kenzo's pleasure-filled torture. Between his fingers and the texture of the towel, Grace found her herself so aroused that she could barely breathe. His kisses on her back and now, at that spot just below her ear was driving her insane. He knew exactly what he was doing to her, and God help her if she didn't mind it one bit. Grace was in such a state that she began moving against him, feeling his hardness, trying to coax him to give both of them the relief they so desperately needed. She pulled forward slightly to turn and face him, but Kenzo held her in place, putting his legs on top of hers. Her limited mobility meant that she had to absorb the pleasure. She could feel her orgasm building against the pressure of the jets. She heard herself moan, felt the clenching of her core, and Kenzo lifted her up slightly and entered her from behind. His hands were at her waist as he moved inside her, feeling her muscles contract against him. Grace leaned forward slightly, and he buried himself inside her. But it wasn't enough for him. He needed to see her face, taste her mouth, her nipples that he knew were swollen from his ministrations.

Huskily, he whispered, "Turn around, baby. I need to see you. I want to see you when you come for me."

Grace almost couldn't comprehend what Kenzo was saying. All she felt was the loss of him inside her. He moved her to face him and she straddled him, easing herself onto him. She felt him pulse within her, and she started moving against him. Grace felt empowered. She wanted to please him as he'd always done for her. She rode him hard, the water splashing between them, her breasts bouncing against his chest. Grace's hands were tightly clamped around his neck as if she was holding on for dear life.

Kenzo placed his left hand against her hip and grabbed Grace's right breast, bringing it to his mouth. He rolled her nipple with his tongue and nipped and sucked it hungrily. She was driving him, and he needed to be driven. He moved his hand from her hip to her breasts, alternating between massaging and sucking on them. He felt her muscles clamp on his manhood, and he knew she was close. And he wasn't too far behind. Grace's moans and ragged breathing intensified as did Kenzo's.

Grace let go of everything and yielded to the pleasure Kenzo was giving her. He was whispering naughty things as his mouth teased her breasts. "That's it, baby. Come for me, Grace." Kenzo thrust upward and moaned with her nipple in his mouth. Grace felt the vibration all the way to her core, and she felt her body shatter. She screamed his name at the same time he released her nipple as he gave into his own release.

"Kenzo!"

"Grace!"

They remained entwined for a few minutes, forehead to forehead, as their breathing normalized. Kenzo rubbed Grace's back lazily.

"Hmmm?" Grace didn't think she possessed the strength to open her eyes. She always needed a moment after they made love. It was all-consuming in a way she'd never known.

"The water's cooled, baby. Let's get you dried off and in bed."

When Grace stood up, she immediately felt the loss of Kenzo's warmth. He grabbed a towel and she stepped out of the whirlpool and stepped inside. He dried her quickly, wrapped her in a towel, and scooped her up and carried her to his bed. He lay behind her, nestling her body into his, and listened for her breathing to slow to let him know she was sleeping before he closed his eyes.

All Grace knew was that she was cold and uncomfortable. She turned over and reached for Kenzo. She'd become accustomed to his warmth surrounding her after their lovemaking. She buried her face into his pillow, inhaling his scent, and suddenly realized that he wasn't there. Her awareness woke her senses. It was still dark, so they hadn't slept that long, just a couple of hours. She heard Miles Davis playing, but she couldn't place the piece. Grace got out of bed and grabbed one of Kenzo's t-shirts to slip on. She was pensive as she descended the stairs. Coltrane was a mellow Kenzo. Miles could mean anything. When she reached the living room, she watched him for a couple of minutes before approaching him. He was wearing a pair of pajama pants that hung low on his hips. Grace couldn't help, even then, to admire how sexy he looked, even in his melancholy mood. She couldn't help but lick her lips at the sight of Kenzo standing there before the large picture window staring into the night. She didn't want to interrupt his private reverie, so she decided to wait.

Kenzo felt her presence when she entered the room, even before he saw her reflection in the glass. He'd known she would come. He watched her through the glass as she stood there, beautifully disheveled in his Jackson State t-shirt that hung mid-thigh on her. Knowing that she was wearing nothing under his shirt aroused him and flooded him with the memories of their lovemaking just hours before. Had he stayed in bed, he would have woken her up to make love to her again, but it would have been a distraction from what he was feeling. That would have been wrong. And the last thing he wanted to do was taint their time that way. He appreciated that she waited, giving him space to decide, and even in the mirror, he could see the range of emotion etched in her features.

Closing his eyes, Kenzo took a deep breath. Without turning around, Kenzo said, "I didn't mean to wake you."

Grace smiled shyly at him, looking at his reflection in the glass, as she walked forward. "Yes, you did, the moment you left the bed." Kenzo still hadn't turned around by the time she'd reached him, but Grace knew he'd been watching her. She put her arms around his waist and lay her cheek on his back. "Do you want to talk?"

Kenzo turned around to face Grace. Resigned, he said, "I suppose we can." "Do you want something to drink?"

"A bottle of water will be fine." Grace followed him to the kitchen and then to the den.

Kenzo sat beside Grace on the sofa but looked straight ahead. He couldn't look at Grace right then. He knew that she was waiting for him and somehow it made it more difficult to begin.

"I need to thank you again for coming today. I know it may seem strange, but you made today bearable. And more than that, I found myself enjoying everything. You made it an experience for me, not an obligation."

"Kenzo, you don't have to..." She was about to say "thank me," but he cut her off.

He turned to her and took her hand. "Let me finish, please. There are some things that I need to just get out. After the groundbreaking, I went to Noelle's grave." Kenzo let them both have a moment to process the gravity of what he'd just said. Kenzo told Grace about his visit and the peace he'd felt. "I told her about you, Grace. I told her I that I'd fallen in love with you."

Kenzo was looking at Grace earnestly, rubbing his thumb gently back and forth on the back of her hand. She exhaled a breath she hadn't known she was holding.

She looked away from him and lowered her head. "Kenzo, I don't know what to say."

Kenzo rubbed her face with the back of his hand and turned her head to him. "You don't have to say anything. You don't have to do anything. I just thought you should know where I stood. But I need to know where you stand too, Grace."

Grace was confused. *How could he not know how she felt?*

Sensing that she didn't understand, Kenzo clarified his statement. "Grace, I didn't say anything earlier, but when I picked you up today, Jaden was there, and we put on quite a show for him. It's clear he came to get you back. I need to know if you want him. I can't play games anymore, or waste time."

If he wasn't so serious in that moment, Grace thought she would have burst into a fit of laughter. But she knew Kenzo was not in the mood for laughter. The seriousness of his expression was clear. Grace took a deep breath and looked him squarely in his gorgeous face.

"When Jaden knocked on my door, the only thing I felt was utter annoyance and disgust. I haven't spoken to him in nearly a year."

"That doesn't mean that you don't love him anymore. You were engaged to the man."

"Kenzo, I realized now that I never really loved Jaden. Our breakup was really a blessing, and to tell the truth, if I'd loved him and he loved me, our breakup never would have happened. He didn't care about who I was beyond him, beyond what I could be for him. I never felt about him the way I feel about you."

Grace and Kenzo said nothing for a few minutes, just looked at each other. Grace decided to break the silence. She knew she needed to say the words that he needed to hear from her.

"I love you, Kenzo. It seems so crazy and so fast, but I do. I..."

She never got a chance to complete the sentence. Kenzo grabbed her and pulled her to him, cupped her face, and slammed his mouth on hers. It was like he was devouring her mouth, and she returned the fervor. Grace's pulse quickened as she felt the waves of desire. She felt his arousal as he continued to consume her mouth from corner to corner. She took a breath when he began nibbling her neck. The sounds of pleasure were inadequate for how he was making her feel, but it was all she could do as his hands roamed over her exposed flesh. Everywhere he touched sent a frisson of heat through her. Her core clenched, and she felt the familiar throbbing that only Kenzo could make her feel. Kenzo's hand travelled beneath the t-shirt she'd thrown on before coming downstairs, as he massaged her breasts, playing with the hardened nipples. It was the most painful of pleasures.

Grace didn't remember when her shirt came off. She couldn't think beyond the way Kenzo had taken hold of her. It was like they couldn't get close enough to each other, couldn't get enough of each other. Grace found herself straddling his lap while he lavished her breasts with his attention. Kenzo still wore his pajama bottoms, but she could feel his hardness. As they moved against each other, she could feel their frustration. Grace decided to take matters into her own hands and slip from his lap. They were both breathing hard, the scent of arousal renting the air. Grace stood between Kenzo's legs. She reached over and put her fingers in the waistband of his pants. Kenzo instinctively lifted himself so she could pull them down.

Kenzo watched Grace. He was as hard as he ever remembered being in his life. Grace stood before him, gloriously nude, and her breasts were still wet from his kisses. Her scent was intoxicating him, and Kenzo knew that he needed to taste her again, be inside her again. And soon. Grace pulled his pants off without taking her eyes from his. He reached for her, but she pulled back slightly and dropped to her knees.

Grace took him into her mouth, slowly, rolling her tongue around the tip of him. Kenzo's sharp inhale and moan was like the sweetest music. She increased the pressure, and he threw his head back against the sofa and groaned in pleasure. He'd dreamed of it but dared not ask. The warmth of her mouth and the vibrations of her moans against him was sheer insanity. Kenzo found his hips moving to her rhythm. He felt the buildup toward a powerful orgasm as Grace increased her fervor. Kenzo needed to be inside of her like he needed his next breath. He reached down and grabbed Grace's arms, and in one swift move, she was beneath him on the sofa. He entered her on a hard thrust, and she arched her back to open herself up to him.

Kenzo took a hardened nipple in his mouth as he moved inside her. It was like he couldn't stop moving, couldn't get inside her deep enough, couldn't taste her enough. Every stroke he gave was returned. Kenzo felt every pulse of her core grip him and hold him captive. Their bodies were frenetic, both of them seeking a new place to hold, to lick, to suck, branding each other with kisses that burned through to the other's soul.

Grace's entire body was on fire. Everywhere Kenzo touched her felt like a trail of fire. No other man could possibly touch her soul so completely. Grace fought against the orgasm building inside her. She didn't want him to stop, she wanted the feel of him inside her as long as possible. But she knew it was useless. Her body wasn't hers anymore. It belonged to him. Kenzo knew her body, knew she was close, and Grace knew one thing for sure, he would shatter her.

Kenzo found his voice somewhere as he felt his orgasm build, and he whispered in her ear between kisses, "You. Are. Mine. Mine. Mine." His voice strained with the impended explosion rising within him, "Come for me, Grace. Come NOW." Grace felt her body shatter into a million pieces. Simultaneously, Kenzo reared his head back as he felt the tremble in his loins and let out a primal yell as he released inside her. His orgasm felt like it would go on forever. Grace's orgasm was pulsating around his shaft, but he still couldn't stop moving inside her. Her scent, the feel of her wetness around him, her cries, strengthened his desire. Kenzo didn't think it was possible, and he couldn't think of anything else.

Kenzo's thrusts became deeper, and he was touching Grace in places that she didn't know existed and had certainly never felt. With her remaining strength, Grace arched her back and felt another orgasm slam into her body. Kenzo took her mouth and devoured her screams just as he came again. He knew in that moment that this is where he belonged.

CHAPTER II

The papers on Grace's desk weren't making any sense. She'd read them over and over, but something was missing. The intelligence she'd received from one of her State Department contacts said that a shipment of girls was arriving on the Gulf Coast. The problem was that her local intel didn't mention a thing about the shipment or who the players were. She still believed in her team, but something was gnawing at her. Something just wasn't right. They should have had this intel first and then confirmed it with the State Department. Not the other way around.

She knew that the East Coast would eventually become trite for traffickers, particularly in the network between Baltimore and New York, and it had. They'd shifted the trade to the southern thoroughfares. Eastern European girls were still a high commodity, because they blended well; however, they blended so well that some could figure out how to leave the pimps and be protected by the police. At the end of the day, they would always be white women—Eastern European or not. But the girls from the Caribbean and Latin countries were cheaper and more afraid of the police. Grace shook her head at the thought. Always a slave trade for black and brown bodies. As many women and girls, and sometimes, boys, she'd liberated, it always hurt a bit more when the bodies looked like her.

Grace checked the time. It was 11:30 a.m. Her team meeting was scheduled for 2:00 p.m., so she had time to grab a bite. She decided to call Treasure to see if she was free. They hadn't talked much lately, and Grace knew that it was as much her fault as it was Treasure's. They hadn't really talked since the reception after the groundbreaking, and Grace still didn't believe Grace's initial explanation that she didn't know Riley Taylor. Something was amiss there as well. And right now, that was the only mystery that she could solve.

Grace waited for Treasure to answer at the shop. She hoped that there was a lull, especially since gala season was over.

"Treasure's Boutique. May I help you?" Treasure's southern lilt drifted over the wires like a true southern belle.

"Hey, Girl. Can you get away for lunch?"

Treasure immediately recognized Grace's voice. She had been dreading this phone call. As much as she loved her best friend in the entire world, Treasure knew that the cop in Grace would rear her ugly head.

"Hi." Her response came out a bit curter than she anticipated. All mirth gone from her business-like voice."

"Treasure? Everything okay?"

Treasure was silent for a split second, and she mustered up some enthusiasm. "Girl, yeah. I was reading over my sales report from my accountant. What's up?"

"I wanted to know if you could get away for a quick bite. I have a meeting at 2, so it would be quick. Can you?"

Treasure was shaking her head "no" but her voice said an enthusiastic "Yes. Want to meet at Walker's?" Walker's wasn't that far from her shop and a short car ride for Grace. She could retreat if necessary. "Let me tell Gena that I'm going out. She can cover the shop while I'm gone."

"Great! See you then."

As Grace clicked off the speakerphone, she frowned. Treasure was behaving strangely, and she had a nagging suspicion that the cause was Riley Taylor. As she walked to the elevator, she decided to call Kenzo. She smiled when he answered on the first ring.

"Hey, Love." Kenzo's voice was so smooth in her ear that she almost forgot why she called.

"Hey, baby. I know you had that big meeting today, but I need to ask you something."

"You know you can ask me anything. What's up?"

"I'm about to have lunch with Treasure. Has RIley said anything about her? You know, they made quite the scene at the reception, and I still don't know why. I was just wondering if Riley had said anything."

"Not a word. Yeah, that was wild. It wasn't like Riley at all. But I don't think he knew her. Riley would have said something to me. Come to think of it, Riley's been out for a couple of days, but he should be in his office today. Want me to say something?"

"Hmmm....interesting." Grace's mind was racing. "No, well, not unless he says something."

"Okay, baby. Dinner tonight?"

"Let me call you. Maybe not dinner, but definitely desert. I promised Mama Hettie that I would have dinner with her."

Kenzo chuckled a bit. "Yes, ma'am. I know I can't compete with Mama Hettie's cooking."

Laughing as she drove into Walker's, "You are crazy, but I'll call you before I leave the office," she replied.

As she hung up the phone, she noted that Treasure hadn't arrived. She parked and waited outside. While she could have checked in for a table, Grace wanted to see her friend arrive, watch her countenance. Grace silently admonished herself for treating her best friend like a suspect, but she couldn't help it. Soon, she saw Treasure. Wearing a yellow maxi dress that hugged her curves and highlighted her bronze skin, Treasure looked like a million dollars. And Grace knew the idiom wasn't too far from the truth. But Grace was trained to see the nuances. As Treasure smiled through the catcalls from the workmen and some of the women working construction, Grace could tell that the smile on Treasure's face faded as soon as it appeared. As Treasure neared the parking lot, Grace exited her car. Both reached the door at the same time.

Grace and Treasure hugged hello, and with a final squeeze, said, "Perfect timing! You look gorgeous."

Treasure, with her smile now at its full wattage, "Why, thank you, darling. Can't own a designer boutique and not look the part! Come on let's get a table and eat. I'm starving."

Grace led the way into the restaurant, so she didn't see the deep breath that Treasure took to calm her nerves or the way in which Treasure's smile seemed to vanish in thin air. Treasure didn't understand her trepidation about meeting her oldest friend for lunch, except that she wanted to avoid all conversation about one Riley Taylor.

After ordering po-boys and catching up on celebrity gossip and some Jackson gossip, the silence that both had been trying to avoid creeped upon them. Treasure realized her mistake as soon as she asked about Kenzo.

Treasure and Grace hadn't talked about the gala, but Treasure figured that she could get Grace to talk about Kenzo, which would keep them occupied until dessert. "So, how's your man?"

"My man?" Grace laughed. As much as she loved him, she wasn't used to the labels yet. "Kenzo's fine. Girl, it's weird. So, here I am, fighting him about the Harrington land one minute, and the next, I'm helping him plan a memorial groundbreaking for his late wife. It sounds crazy as hell."

Treasure took a sip of her iced tea. "Yeah, it does. It's been five years, is he ready to move on? I mean, most men are re-married in a year, but Kenzo didn't date, didn't go out, hadn't been seen with a woman....until you. You have no idea the phone calls and death threats I made to keep your name out folks' mouths!"

Grace and Treasure were laughing so hard that they couldn't even acknowledge the waiter who took their plates away. It was girlish, infectious laughter that had them dabbing at the tears in their eyes with napkins.

"I bet you did. Girl, the first night we just went to a business dinner, tongues were wagging. I wondered about it myself, whether he was ready to move on, but I think the groundbreaking and the reception made it final. I mean, he says he's ready. So, for now, I have to trust that."

The waiter returned to refill their glasses, and as Grace reached for a packet of sweetener, she looked at Treasure, ready to discuss the elephant at the table.

"So, what happened, Treasure?"

Taking a sip of her tea, Treasure feigned ignorance. "What do you mean?"

Grace's eyebrow raised. "Girl. You and Riley. That was no first meeting. I let you make it that night, but we've been friends too long for you to lie and even still, for you to think I would believe it."

Treasure hung her head. When she lifted it again, she'd decided to tell her friend the truth. "I met Riley one night for dinner, and it was awful. A friend of mine suggested that we meet, and we did. At first, I thought he was fine as hell. You know how I feel about a six-footer with a broad back."

Both women laughed. Grace chucked, "Yes, girl, I know. I remember, Adonis Collier from high school. You were completely sprung on that one."

"Yes, Indeed." Treasure clutched her fake pearls and waved a white napkin in full southern belle mode. "Well, anyway, as fine as Riley was, he was arrogant and so cocky that he turned me completely off. All he could talk about was himself and his business. He thought my boutique was playing dress-up."

Grace took a sharp inhale, "No, he didn't..."

Treasure always become angry when someone disrespected her and definitely her business. "I didn't know who he thought he was, but I wasn't there for that. Okaaaay!"

"So, the date ended, and you never saw him again until the gala?"

"Not exactly." Treasure looked away from Grace's questioning eyes to collect her thoughts. "Remember when I was staying at the Hilton while my floors were being installed and the house painted?

Grace nodded.

"Well, I was staying at the Hilton then. Riley brought me back to the Hilton, and..."

Grace cut her off, "Wait. The date was terrible, right? Don't tell me. Y'all? How? And why haven't you told me? Lord."

"Let me finish. One question at a time, ma'am. Yes, all of that. But on the ride over to the Hilton, he got a call from his sister who put his niece on the phone. At first, I was irritated that he took the call, especially since he hadn't said two words to me, but Grace, it was the sweetest thing. He was still arrogant, but softer. The niece, she had to be four or five, was asking him about coming to his house the next weekend, and what all they were going to do. And it was like he was a different person. If I had met that Riley at dinner, then I wouldn't have ordered the cheesecake."

Grace laughed. Treasure continued, "When he clicked off the call, I must have been staring at him, and it was like he remembered I was in the car. I told him that I thought it was sweet for him to spend time with his niece. And then he starts talking about his sister and her children, and he was like a completely different person. He has two nephews, but that little girl wanted to spend the weekend with her uncle. I thought, he couldn't be that bad, right? All the talking we should have done at dinner was had as he walked me to my room."

"Next thing I knew, my clothes were off, and we were going at it. It was the best sex I've ever had, but just because we were good together in bed didn't mean that we were compatible. So, we decided to enjoy our weekend, keep it between us, and leave Monday morning with no regrets. And that's what we did."

"So, why the anger then the other night at the reception?"

"Because I had been avoiding Riley for the last three years, and then you go and fall in love with his business partner." Treasure threw her hands up the air. "And by that Monday morning, I changed my mind."

Grace looked at her friend. She saw something she'd never seen before. Pain. "You changed your mind? Did you want more than he was willing to give?"

"I didn't tell him. That Monday, he sent flowers with a standard player's card, and I never heard from him again. So that's that." Treasure played with her napkin, waiting for Grace to say something.

Grace placed her hand over Treasure's. "You fell hard, didn't you?"

Treasure nodded, "I thought I was over it, but seeing him brought it all back. And he smelled so good that night. Elevators shouldn't be that small."

Grace patted Treasure's hand. "So, what are you going to do? What if we're all together again? Do you still want him? If so, you need to tell him how you feel. He might feel differently too even after all this time."

Treasure laughed. "That player? Child, please. "I'll be fine. Just needed to get over the shock. I'm cool now. Trust. He will not rattle me again."

Treasure didn't believe a word coming out of her mouth. And neither did Grace.

For the first time in her career, Grace didn't fully feel confident in her team.

As they discussed the intel she'd received, she realized that they had no idea how bad things could really get. Trafficking was big business, and she realized that they didn't really have a clue as to what the numbers really meant. She chewed on the top of her pen as she studied them. It wasn't entirely their fault, really, because small cities like Jackson were just coming to understand. Had she not spent the early part of her career in the field, she probably wouldn't know either. Grace knew they had big fish to bait and hook this time. The coffle was arriving in a few weeks, and she had to get them ready—psychologically and emotionally for the characters they would have to play. And she knew she would have to suit up—literally.

"Listen, this intel is solid, and I know the traffickers are landing on the coast. I'm still waiting to hear the other details of the shipment, but it looks like we'll be spending some quality time on the Coast. We need to establish a presence, hit the private games at the casinos, and listen."

Terry was skeptical. "So, we just move to the Coast for a few weeks, throw some money around, and the traffickers will seek us out." She could tell that the others were thinking the same thing but were afraid to ask.

"That about sums it up. As soon as I get more concrete details, we will establish new identities and scenarios. This isn't a "drugs on the table" operation. We follow the money. Period. And I'll be taking lead. What I know they don't expect, at least in Mississippi, is a female and a black one at that running the game. Edward and Zara, go back to the Darknet. See if there's any chatter that sounds promising regarding this area or the South, in general. Sometimes, they'll spread the girls in surrounding states to create a new network. In the meantime, prepare yourselves and your families. They won't know where you are or where you've gone. It's safer that way. Trust me."

As everyone closed their folders, Grace's assistant, Deloria, walked in. She made an immediate beeline to Grace and whispered in her ear. "There's a man on the phone."

Grace didn't know if she was irritated with her team or Deloria more at that moment. But she tried to keep her emotions in check. "Yes? Did he give you a name?"

Deloria shook her head. Through a forced whisper, Deloria said, "He wouldn't say. But said that he needed to speak to you now. He was quite rude."

"I'll handle it, Deloria. Thank you." Grace turned to her team, who had been lingering at the door, "Hold on, let's see if this is the call I've been waiting on."

Grace picked up the receiver. "Grace Harrington."

"Meet me at 5:00 in the train station on Mill Street. And tell no one, not even the five people looking at you right now." The line clicked. She recognized the voice on the other end immediately, but Grace knew the drill, pretense had become her middle name. She tried to fix her feature as to not give anything away. "Hello? Hello?" Still holding the receiver, Grace said to her audience, "Guess whoever it was hung up."

Terry was the last to leave the room. He stared at Grace for a moment before adding, "Don't know who would have scared Deloria like that, but whoever it was didn't hang up. So, whenever you're ready, you'll let us know." Without waiting for her to respond, he turned and left the room.

———

Grace was at the train station at 4:45. She always kept a change of clothes at the office, so she put on a jogging suit and decided that a run to the train station would be excellent cover. No one would pay any attention to her exercising, she hoped. The train station was minutes from her office, so she could run there and back. She could blend in with the crowd.

When she arrived at the station, she bought a water bottle from the gift shop and scanned the waiting room for an available seat. As she'd expected, no one paid her any attention. For all they knew, she was just taking a break from running like the new inhabitants of downtown, or even getting on the 5:45 train to Chicago. Most were seated in the first two benches near the door, dropping their bags and themselves in the first available seat they could find. She was early, but took a seat in the corner at the rear wall. The only other person in the area was an old white man reading the paper. Plus, it was easier to see the door from that angle and wait for the voice she knew.

As soon as she sat down, the old man peered from behind his paper.

"You're late, Gracie."

The voice didn't match the face staring back at her, but he couldn't hide those piercing eyes. She rolled her eyes. "I'm not late, Chief, I'm early. You've just been here since three o'clock." The benches were close enough so that they could speak freely for a while, but Chief moved slowly to her side anyway.

Chief had been her training agent when she started going undercover. He was a master of disguises and accents. He'd worked hard at the Department when there weren't but a few blacks in the field. And when the CIA's Dark Web was overrun with illegal operations, he'd been tasked to investigate. What could have been a suicide mission for his career turned into their specialized unit. Chief was a hard man, but they were both from the South; he was from Alabama, a small town named Butler, on the Mississippi line. He'd taken her under his wing and taught her how to navigate the Department and the work without losing her soul. Chief taught her what wasn't in the textbooks and the knowledge had saved her life on more occasions than she cared to remember.

As calmly as she could and without looking at him, Grace asked, "What are you doing here and as white no less? How in the world?"

"You know I rarely come South without the complexion for the protection." Chief hated the South. It was one of the few things on which they disagreed, but Grace knew that whatever horrors he'd seen growing up in Jim Crow Alabama were indelibly imprinted on his soul.

"Lord, man."

"Heard you got some intel."

"Yeah, a shipment on the Coast. It's good, right?"

"Oh, yeah, your intel is solid. Your team ain't."

Grace froze. She hissed, "What do you mean, my team isn't solid?"

Chief turned the newspaper's pages. The sound of the rustling paper grating on her nerves. Chief was going to prolong this. "Don't know who it is, but that intel had been floating for weeks. Someone held it from you. Don't know which one."

Grace closed her eyes. Something was definitely off and had been for a while, except she'd been caught up. Distracted.

"That fella you're seeing have something to do with the fact that you got a mole and don't know it?"

Grace kept silent. The last thing she wanted was for him to be right and for it to be true.

"You were engaged to Jaden for a year and never lost focus like this. This must be serious."

"It is. But I won't let it interfere with the work."

Chief looked at her directly and sighed. "Oh, grasshopper," his eyes softening a bit. "It already has."

Grace wanted to respond but couldn't. She knew he was right, and Grace knew that she needed laser focus. She could plan a million operations, but just how she was going to stay away from Kenzo, she had absolutely no idea. But she had a larger problem. A mole. Chief was never wrong about these things, but she had to find out who was sabotaging the task force.

Chief rustled his newspaper again, and Grace knew that the conversation was over. Grace got up from the bench and walked away without a further word.

───────

Kenzo was leaning against Grace's car when she returned from the train station. Even from a distance, he could see that her jaw was set hard, her delectable mouth in a determined pout. She was mad, and he hoped that he wasn't the cause, because whoever caused this look on his woman's face was in real trouble. His woman. Kenzo liked the sound of that in his head and smiled in her direction. As he waited, he took a moment to study her movements. Grace moved effortlessly, even in her anger, and she was still as gorgeous as when she was smiling. But right now, she damn sure wasn't smiling. Kenzo felt it the moment she recognized that it was him standing there, and his arms opened for her.

When Grace's mind recognized that it was Kenzo standing at her car, she broke into a sprint to him. All she could see was him, standing there, waiting for her. She nearly knocked him down when she barreled into to him. She didn't know she was cold until his embrace warmed her. Grace held him tightly, inhaling his scent and basking in the feel of being held by the man she loved. After a few moments, Kenzo whispered her name, "Grace. Baby, what's wrong? You're trembling."

Grace couldn't speak. She lifted her head and stared into Kenzo's eyes. She couldn't speak, and she needed to be away from there. Luckily, she'd already put her things in the car. She didn't want to go to the office. Grace didn't want to be on the premises one more second.

"I need to get out of here. Now. Just take me home."

Kenzo's brow raised. He'd never seen Grace so upset. He ran his fingers through her hair, bent his head, and captured her mouth. The kiss was sweet but definitely too short. "You're too upset to drive. My car?"

Grace nodded, and she immediately felt the loss when she left the comfort of Kenzo's arms. Grabbing her briefcase and purse from her trunk, she walked to Kenzo's car, which was, thankfully, parked a few spaces from hers in the parking lot. Kenzo opened her car door, and before she eased into the seat, she caught a last glimpse of the sun as it descended and the rise of the moon. How appropriate, she thought. She slid onto the leather seat and closed her eyes just as Kenzo closed the car door.

Kenzo didn't say another word as he started the car and pulled out of the lot. He knew that she would share when she was ready. As he rode down Capitol Street, Kenzo stole a few glances at Grace. Her eyes were closed, but her fists were balled so tight that her knuckles were white. He reached over and placed his hand over her left hand until she relaxed her hand enough to allow him to slip his fingers through hers. Kenzo lifted their now joined hands to his lips and kissed the back of her hand. They rode in silence, neither saying a word, even after Kenzo pulled into his garage and killed the engine. Kenzo grabbed her bag and handed Grace her purse from the backseat and led her into the house. As soon as he entered the living room, he grabbed the remote, and soon, the sounds of Dinah Washington's "What a Difference a Day Makes" filled the room.

Grace took a seat on the sofa trying to gather her thoughts and what she could say to him in a few moments that would make any of what she needed to say okay.

Kenzo finally broke the silence. "Here. Looks like you need it." He'd handed her a glass of red wine, her favorite Argentinian Malbec. Grace took the glass and quickly took a sip. She let the wine dance on her tongue. Perhaps, it would help loosen her up. She still didn't know what to feel, but she felt safe enough now to feel something...even if she didn't know what it was.

After a few moments, Grace told Kenzo about Chief and his information. Kenzo laughed about Chief's old white man disguise, which made her laugh. But eventually the reality set in that she had a mole on her team that she didn't detect.

Kenzo asked, "So, you trust Chief's information?"

Grace quickly responded, "I trust Chief with my life. So, yes, I trust it because I trust him."

Kenzo nodded and swirled his remaining wine in his glass. He watched the red liquid coat the sides of the glass, and after a moment, looked up and saw Grace staring at him. "That's not all, Grace. That's not enough to have gotten you that upset. What else is there?"

This was the moment she dreaded. "I should have known, and I didn't. I carefully selected my team. I vetted their credit and their vices to ensure that no one could be bought. And I clearly missed something." The next sentence out of her mouth came fast and on one breath. "And I missed it because I was distracted."

Kenzo understood immediately. "I see. So, I am a distraction." He was hurt and angry. He swirled the wine in his glass again and swallowed all of the remaining wine.

"Yes, a wonderful, beautiful distraction, but one nevertheless." Grace's eyes were searching Kenzo's. "I have to focus all my energies now on finding out the mole and planning this operation. I can't have any distractions, Kenzo. This is too important."

Kenzo rose from his seat on the sofa and poured himself another glass. Grace continued, "You know what's at stake, Kenzo. Not just for Jackson, but for me, too." She heard the pleading in her voice, but Kenzo hadn't turned around to look at her. He was methodically pouring his glass, taking his time, gathering his thoughts and devising his approach. Grace was a woman, his woman, and she was scared; and before he let her put some distance between them just when he had let her into his heart, he would do what he had to do. He decided to pivot the conversation a bit. He returned to the sofa and sat next to her, angling his body so that she would do the same.

"Tell me about the operation you're planning."

Grace knew what Kenzo was doing, but she played along anyway. They were both stalling, trying to avoid the inevitable—at least for a while. She told him that a trailer shipment of girls was heading to the Gulf Coast soon, and she would be leaving to set up her operation.

"Do you understand what I'm telling you, Kenzo? I need to be incommunicado for a few weeks. No distractions. Plus, I don't want you in harm's way. Whoever is close to me is a target. And that means you and Mama Hettie. I'm going to send her to my folks' place as a gift, so she won't be here. I never told her about the nature of what I really do, and I don't plan to start now."

Kenzo set his glass down slowly. He wanted to laugh, but he knew that she was serious. Grace expected him to go along with this. But that simply was not going to happen.

"Where are your folks, now? And you think Hettie Harrington is going to leave Jackson...on your say so?"

"Thankfully, my dad is stationed in the South Pacific. I'll call him tomorrow. Hawaii will be a nice vacation for Mama Hettie." Grace sighed and looked away. For the first time, she wanted the mundanity of a vacation without seeing crime and inhumanity everywhere.

Kenzo rose from his spot on the sofa, pulled her up with him, and brought her close to his body. He held her close, rubbing her back. He could feel the tension between her shoulder blades. As much as he didn't want to, he pulled back slightly so he could see her face.

"So, you're not angry with me but at yourself. You think being with me has become a distraction?"

Grace nodded, her eyes watering with tears. "Kenzo, I've worked so hard to get to where I am, and this is an opportunity I can't waste right now." She looked back down, unable to look into the depths of concern in his eyes.

Kenzo gently took hold of her chin and forced her to look at him.

"Don't you know that I wouldn't do anything to hurt you or your career? But let's get one thing straight, love. There is no way you're going to escape me, or us, that easily." When she tried to look away, Kenzo held her firmly in place. She was frustratingly stubborn, but that only added to her appeal for him. He placed his forehead on hers and softly murmured against her skin, "Let's go upstairs."

Grace knew that going upstairs was a bad idea. She knew exactly where it would lead, but the problem wasn't going away. She needed to put her relationship on ice, if only for a little while. But there was something in her that needed these final moments with him. She needed clarity, to be released from the tension in her mind and spirit. Grace knew that Kenzo would relieve her of all of it, even if it would return in the morning. Because then, she would have to say goodbye to Kenzo, deal with the mole in her unit and plan the sting of her career.

Grace felt her body moving. Kenzo was leading her upstairs, her hand in his. His warmth was travelling through her like a trembling stream. Grace felt each step as they ascended the staircase, and she tried to convince herself that she could get through the night and walk away the next morning.

Kenzo led her to the bedroom and deposited her on the bed.

"Wait here. I'll run a bath for you."

Grace sat silent and watched him from her point on the bed. She could see his reflection in the glass as he leaned over and adjusted the water's temperature. As the water was running, she watched him place towels on the warmer. She smiled in spite of how she was feeling. Kenzo was the most caring man she'd ever met. He knew just what to do to take care of her.

When the water finished running, Kenzo placed a few droplets of various oils in the bathwater. Satisfied that everything was ready, Kenzo returned to Grace and led her to the bath. Without a word between them, Kenzo undressed Grace, his eyes never leaving hers, except to remove her pants. Grace placed her hands on his shoulders for balance, and Kenzo felt the weight of what she was feeling through her hands. She was gripping him tightly as if she was trying to hold on to him, to the moments between them. Kenzo rose and gave her a chaste kiss. Anything deeper and he knew that he would be in the bath with her. That's not what she needed right now, and it was taking everything in him to stay focused.

As Kenzo helped her into the tub, Grace realized that Kenzo wasn't joining her. "You're not coming in with me?"

Kenzo laughed softly and kissed her forehead, "No, love. This is for you, not me."

Grace almost fought a full-fledged pout. "But..."

Kenzo cut her off. "Trust me."

Grace lowered herself into the bathtub and inhaled. "What did you put in here? It smells like heaven."

"Lavender and Frankincense."

"Frankincense as in gift to Jesus, Frankincense?"

"Yes, it helps with relaxation, especially when mixed with lavender."

"Hmm...yes it does."

Kenzo handed her the washcloth and kissed her softly on the lips. "Call me when you're ready to get out." When she leaned her head back and closed her eyes, Kenzo eased out of the bathroom and closed the door.

Kenzo headed downstairs to his office to make a quick phone call. He called Marcus, giving him the names of all of Grace's team members. He told Marcus that he didn't just want their histories, he wanted lineage. Someone on her team had been compromised, and most likely money was involved. He needed the financials of the team and all of their relatives. Kenzo pressed the urgency of the situation to Marcus and ended the call. He poured a glass of wine and thought about who the mole could be. Marcus never failed him before, but he definitely couldn't fail him this time. He needed to find out who it was before Grace's sting.

Kenzo returned to the bathroom and smiled at the woman sleeping in his bathtub. The water was lukewarm, but the aroma of the oils still lingered.

"Grace." Kenzo really didn't want to wake her, but he knew he had to do so.

Grace heard Kenzo from a remote place in her mind call her name. Her limbs were completely relaxed as was her mind. She didn't respond at first. She couldn't. Or perhaps, she wanted to hear him call her name again.

"Grace. Love. It's time to get out of the bath."

Grace lazily opened her eyes. She would never get tired of looking at those almond eyes that held so much passion and love in them. He was almost like a mirage, but he was very real. He held out a fluffy and warm towel, and after a long, appreciative moment, Grace decided to stand up.

Kenzo took in a sharp inhale. The oils had given her an ethereal glow, and Grace was standing before him more beautiful than any woman he'd ever seen. She walked into the towel and his embrace, and he patted her dry, preserving the oils in her skin. As he did so, neither of them said a word. When he finished, he picked a second towel from the warmer, wrapped her in it, and picked her up to carry her to his bed.

Grace never felt so cared for in her life. Kenzo placed her gently on the bed and knelt before her, drying her feet. When he was finished, he cocooned her in the down comforter, sealing her in warmth.

Kenzo walked to the other side of the bed and got undressed. He slid behind her and brought her into his body, her head resting in the crook of his arm. Grace fit him perfectly in so many ways, and Kenzo placed a kiss on the back of her head. Grace's breathing was already measured and even, letting Kenzo know that she was in a deep sleep. Good. He lay there listening and enjoying her being there with him and relishing the fact that he was the one who brought her some peace. Experience taught him the hard way that you never know how much time you have with the people you love. But he knew two things for sure. Someone was after his woman. And he was going to find out who.

CHAPTER 12

Grace closed the folder on her desk. Within two weeks, she'd moved out of Mama Hettie's, packed her off to Hawaii, and planned what she hoped was an operation that would capture a few bad guys. She'd decided to move into the adjoining residential space at the office. She knew that Kenzo was none too pleased with her, especially after she'd turned down his offer to stay with him. But she knew that she needed focus and living with Kenzo was not only going to make her lose all kinds of focus, but also put him in harm's way. Grace shook her head. Kenzo didn't press her too hard, but she knew he didn't fully understand what kind of people she was chasing.

On top of that, she still hadn't uncovered who the traitor was in her office. She suspected Luther, but just couldn't be sure. She double-checked everyone's history to see if there was anything that she'd missed, but she still found nothing, which was frustrating her even more. Grace turned from her desk to face the window. The sun was shining, and it seemed a beautiful day. From her vantage point, the cars and people looked like ants. She watched them mill about, unaware of the dangers surrounding them. She envied their innocence and benign self-centeredness. And just once, she wanted a piece of that for herself. It's why, Grace thought, she left the State Department, why she came home. It was never the job that exhausted her. It was the inhumanity, and now, in Jackson, she couldn't trust her own people.

Grace rested her head against her chair, closed her eyes, and let out a long exhale. Grace knew she needed a good night's sleep. She hadn't been sleeping well between her issues at work and with Kenzo. But sleeping in her chair, as comfortable as it is to sit in, wasn't going to cut it. Grace rose and walked over to the sofa in her office. Perfect. Deloria was still out front and wouldn't disturb her.

I just need twenty minutes, Grace thought. *A power nap and I'll get back at it.* Grace set the alarm on her phone, lay out on the sofa, and drifted off to sleep.

Kenzo stood in the doorway of Grace's office watching her sleep. She looked so peaceful that he decided to just write her a note and let her know he'd been there. He didn't want to disturb her, but he'd been disturbed for the past couple of weeks. He missed her like he'd never missed anyone. He hadn't had a full night's sleep in days, tortured by the memories of the last time they'd made love. And he simply missed her. He missed her in his kitchen. He missed watching her enjoying a good movie or even a bad one. He missed her laughter. She'd filled every gaping hole in his life with love and a peace he hadn't known in a long time. He walked toward her, careful not to wake her, but close enough to satisfy himself. Even when she was sleeping, she was beautiful. He looked down at her and wondered if he could steal just one kiss without waking her up. He sighed, knowing that one wouldn't be enough. He'd want more, and that *would* disturb her.

Resigned, he walked toward her desk to write a note to her, but just as he was about to place the note on her desk, he heard her whisper his name. Kenzo smiled. She was dreaming about him. He couldn't help but feel a sense of pride at the knowledge that she missed him as much as he was missing her. Kenzo felt the urge to wake her, put them both out of this misery of loneliness. As Kenzo made his way to her, he watched her face begin to contort in a frown and her breathing become erratic. *Her dream of him was turning into a nightmare?* She called his name again, nearly frantic, in her sleep. Kenzo rushed to her side and knelt beside her.

"Grace. Love. Wake up." He kissed her softly, gently nudging and rubbing her shoulder to wake her. She responded to his touch, but her breathing was still ragged. He was amused and worried at the same time. He didn't realize how worried she had been. A woman who had taken down sex cartels in Europe was worried about him.

Grace opened her eyes slowly and upon seeing Kenzo, started blinking furiously. When Grace realized that Kenzo was kneeling before her, she tried to speak but couldn't seem to form a coherent thought. "K-K-Kenzo. What? Why?" She sat up and Kenzo sat next to her. He looked amazing in his Armani suit, and Grace breathed in his scent. He was too close to her, and Grace knew she couldn't keep a level head around him. The dream was proof of that.

Kenzo laughed. "Well, I saw that you hadn't left, and even though I know you needed space, I just wanted to see you. I won't bother you long, I promise. I wasn't going to wake you, just leave a note, but you called for me. And then it seemed that you were having a nightmare. It must have been some dream you were having." Kenzo pulled her to him, and she felt good nestled into his body. A perfect fit.

Grace studied her hands, one of which was in his. "I missed you, too. It's been a long two weeks, and texting and a few phone calls just made it worse. And I appreciate that you understood my position. Most men wouldn't have. But I needed this time."

"I know you did. I just needed to see you today. Deloria waved me in, but don't be mad at her. Perhaps, I came in the nick of time. Tell me about your dream."

Grace paused for a moment. "I missed you too, and that's how the dream started. But then somehow you were taken from me, and I couldn't find you." Grace didn't want to tell him that, somehow, he had gotten in the crossfire, but she knew the dream was a warning. She needed to finish this operation, and he needed to stay away from her. *But, Lord, it feels so good to be in his arms again.*

Kenzo kissed Grace's temple. "Love, I really just came to see you and maybe get a kiss to get me through the night." As much as he didn't want to, Kenzo was disciplined to know that the longer he stayed, the more he was at risk of breaking his promise. She was smelling too good, and it had been too long. Kenzo had to laugh at himself. After five years of celibacy, two weeks without Grace in his bed was killing him.

He rose and pulled her up with him. "So, may I have my kiss?"

He smiled at her as he put his arms around her waist. Grace was almost prepared to throw caution to the wind, but she was glad he had more control than she. She placed her arms around his neck, and Kenzo lowered his mouth to hers. The moment he kissed her, Grace's entire body heated, and she knew she wanted more. *What was she thinking?* She'd told her entire team to spend as much time with the people they loved, and yet, here she was punishing herself and him, for that matter. She deepened the kiss, and Kenzo pulled back. But Grace kissed him with a determined fervor. After a moment, Kenzo tightened his hold on her. Grace could feel his desire for her, and like always, her body responded in kind. Her nipples tightened, and she rubbed her body against his. Anything to get closer, to create the friction she needed for release.

All of the control Kenzo thought he had disappeared the moment he kissed her. He was drowning in her kiss, and she wasn't making it easy on either of them. When they came up for air, both of them were breathing hard. The air around them sizzled with sexual energy and desire. Kenzo placed his forehead on Grace's. Her breathing was just as ragged as his.

"Baby, please," Kenzo said, in a hoarse whisper. "I'm strong, but you're killing me. I need to go."

Grace lay her head directly over Kenzo's heart and realized his heartbeat matched her own. She held him tighter. "No, you don't. Come with me."

"That's not what I came here for."

"I know." Grace was kissing him again, placing kisses around his mouth and his neck. In between kisses, she said, "But you're here now. I'm here."

"Damn, woman." Kenzo took in a sharp inhale when she placed her hands beneath his shirt and ran her fingernails across his back. He had no resistance to this or her. He was harder than he'd ever been, and he needed to be inside her like he needed to breathe. He slammed his mouth on hers and kissed her hard. He held the back of her neck with one hand while the other was unbuttoning her blouse. He felt her hardened nipples though the lace of her bra. Kenzo stopped kissing her long enough to admire her perfect breasts and groaned when he saw her purple lace bra against her skin. When he looked up, Grace was looking at him, her eyes blazing with desire.

"Don't move, Love." Kenzo quickly walked over to the door and locked it, silently cursing himself for not locking it in the first place.

Grace stood there, watching him. She was so turned on that she wanted to weep. Satisfied that they wouldn't be disturbed, Kenzo kissed her while moving them to the sofa. He sat and pulled her on top of him so that she was straddling his legs. They looked at each other for a moment, and Kenzo pushed an errant curl from her face. "You are so beautiful, Grace." He traced the outline of her bra with his finger. Grace trembled. No man had loved her so completely and passionately. He popped the front clasp of her bra and her breast sprang free.

He cupped both in his hands, massaging them first before he took a hardened bud in his mouth. He massaged one breast while he sucked the nipple and kissed the other. Grace's skirt was pushed up to the tops of her thighs. Still torturing her breasts, Kenzo moved his hands up her thighs until he found the silk of her panties. He rubbed the silky material first, and then moved the scrap of fabric so his could explore her core. "Baby, you're drenched. You ready for me?" Grace forced out a moan-filled "yes" amidst the sensations Kenzo was making her feel.

Kenzo needed to be inside of Grace now. Knowing how ready she was for him, the scent of her was driving him insane. Kenzo licked her essence from his fingers and gently pushed her off him and removed her skirt and his clothes. He wanted to taste her completely, but it would have to wait. He brought her back on top of him, and the second he'd entered her warmth, he almost lost all control. Grace was riding him hard and slow at the same time, and Kenzo felt Grace's muscles grip him. He never felt anything like this before in his life. Grace picked up the pace, and Kenzo latched on to her breasts, nibbling and sucking both with fervor. Grace never felt so full and complete, and she knew her orgasm was close and so was his. At the same time, Grace and Kenzo looked at each other, and the looks of love and desire were enough to push both of them over the edge. Grace trembled in his hands and she felt his seed pour into her like molten lava. Kenzo captured her mouth just as she came, swallowing their moans as they rode the power of their orgasm into bliss.

Grace tried to ease herself from Kenzo's lap, but he wouldn't let her go. She still felt him inside her, partially erect. She lay her head in the crook of his neck as he caressed her back. Grace wondered if their lovemaking would always be like this, so overwhelming and passionate. She didn't want to move, but she knew she couldn't have this conversation in this position, not with him inside her and touching her like this.

"I've got to get up, baby."

Kenzo groaned as she lifted herself. Grace felt the loss of him immediately, as she always did. She decided to just rip the band-aid off.

"I leave in two days." She held her breath, waiting for him to respond.

Kenzo felt the tension ripple through her. "Do you have everything you need? Everything's in place?"

Grace nodded. "Yes, the team left days ago to meet and set everything up." Before she could caution herself, she told him the details. "I'm using one of my aliases from the State Department. Chief has a separate team down there since we haven't been able to detect who the mole is." Grace was still embarrassed by that fact. Chief hadn't been able to figure it out either, and he and Grace debated calling the whole thing off but going forward was the only way to find out who it was.

Kenzo said, "Will you give me the next two days then?" It was part question, part plea. He didn't know what was going to happen, didn't want to think about it, but he'd learned the hard way to seize every possible moment.

Grace didn't need a moment to think. "Yes."

CHAPTER 13

Zara pulled out her burner cell phone and dialed a number. She hated herself and even more, she hated her father for putting her in a position to betray everything she believed in. Zara was still angry that he could gamble while her mother was fighting for her life. Her mother couldn't help being sick, but he could have stopped himself. Gotten some help. Not made deals with the Devil. As the phone rang, she fingered the ring that she wore, the one they made her wear, that would identify her. Grace was scheduled to arrive later that day, but Zara and the team would have no communication with her until just before showtime.

The shipment of girls was slated to arrive that morning, and Grace was to pose as a buyer at an undisclosed location that evening. Edward and Terry had infiltrated the network online and secured an invitation to the auction that evening. The girls would be auctioned off to the highest bidder, even categorized by age and experience. The virgins would command a higher price, the younger, the better. Grace had tried to explain to her team the horrors that she'd seen all over Europe, but Zara didn't think she was ready to see a child being auctioned off like a slave. If all went well, Grace would make the purchase and the team and the Feds would move in for the arrest. But Zara knew that wasn't going to be the case. Grace would never make the auction.

As much as she hated that and herself, Zara had to save her family first.

The drive to the Coast was a hard one. She and Kenzo had a beautiful two days, and he walked her to her car, loaded her bags, and kissed her. Kenzo never offered to come with her, nor did he ask her to drop the entire thing. Their good-bye was sweet with "be careful's" and "I love you's." She finally had to break the spell and get in the car and drive off. She promised to call when it was all over, and she was on her way back. She even joked about having oxtails and rice for her first meal home. The cloud of whether she was coming back hung over them, but neither of them acknowledged it. She smiled at him as she drove off, waving at him like she was going to the store.

Grace arrived in Biloxi in two hours. Rather than go to the hotel where she would be staying, she had prearranged to meet with Chief in the neighboring city of Pass Christian. Chief had been watching her back and her team since they arrived, trying to determine the mole. They had combed through financials of all her team members and their families, and not one red flag popped up. She knew that Zara's mother had medical bills but there had been no lump sum payments, nor had there been with anyone else. Grace pulled up to a non-descript, white frame house. A beat-up truck was parked in the yard, and a sleeping dog lay on the porch in front of the door.

As she approached the door, Chief opened the door and walked further into the house. She closed and locked the door, following him. He handed Grace a steaming mug of coffee and plopped down in a chair. He pulled no punches.

"Your mole is protected."

"Protected by whom?" Her brain was racing.

"Whoever is facilitating this auction. The financials all came up normal. What I did find out was that you are the primary target."

Grace's face went to stone. She'd made her enemies in her arrest, but the Department had protected her true identity. *How would anyone have tracked her here, to Mississippi, to Jackson?* Though she trusted Chief, a part of her was incredulous, and she had to ask, "How? What's the intel?"

Chief looked at Grace. She'd become like a daughter to him. She was green when she came into the department, but she was strong, teachable, and smarter than some of his more experienced agents. He brought his mug to his lips and took a healthy swig. "Remember that operation in Paris?"

"Of course. My first as lead, but that whole ring was taken down. Everyone involved was either killed in the takedown, or jailed."

"Not everyone. Remember the son of Amir Hassem?"

Grace nodded. Little Amir was twelve when she arrested his father. And his father thought it was appropriate to bring him to the auction so he could choose a mistress. It made Grace sick to her stomach.

"He remembered you. For the last fifteen years, he and his mother have been looking for you. You, grasshopper, have a target on your back."

"Well, damn." Grace shook her head. This is crazy, she thought, but she was slightly pleased. Her work had been impactful enough that they had followed her halfway around the world. She looked at Chief squarely. "Let's get to it then. I'm ready."

Grace checked into the dummy hotel in Gulfport and summoned her team. She surveyed each member of her team, listening to their voices as they went over the details, watching their eyes for any tells. She saw nothing except that Zara and Edward were nervous. Grace, though, chalked it up to their first major bust. She remembered what she was like her first time out. But still, Edward's nervous energy was masked in a cowboy persona. Cowboys usually made mistakes, and since she didn't know if he was the saboteur, she had to watch him closely. Terry was calm. Almost too calm. But then, so was she, surprisingly so, after learning that she was targeted for a hit. The auction was scheduled in a week, so this would be their last meeting.

Edward and Terry had made the contacts weeks ago and were waiting on the final instructions. Even though they knew the day, the time and place would be kept secret until the very last minute. Since Chief was running a shadow team, she knew his team would receive the same instructions. In the next two days, Grace and Zara would work the casinos and the high-end nightlife of the Coast. All of them were listening and watching the high rollers, the talkers, and the silent ones. The silent ones always gave her pause. Those were the ones who were really in charge.

Grace and Zara checked into the penthouse suite at the Beau Rivage and spent the days pretending to shop and pamper themselves, while their nights were filled with private gambling rooms both at the casinos and private residences. The fellas did the same, throwing money around at the casinos, golf courses, and strip clubs. Thank God, they didn't have to do it long, or neither one would be able to go back home.

Once Grace was in character, that's who she became. This alias played hard and had a nasty attitude toward everyone. Educated, spoiled, and used to getting what she wanted, Grace embodied Parminder Anwar, a British-educated, Arabian princess. She shooed hotel staff away, gritted her teeth at perceived incompetence, and even made selfish demands of the concierge and hotel staff. Grace could only tolerate this part because she knew that it was part of the operation and it wasn't her. This was the job.

The first time, Zara saw Grace's Parminder she was amazed at how deeply she was entrenched in the character. Zara was supposed to be playing an equally snobbish character, but even she knew it felt forced. Grace had to step out of Parminder when they were alone to give her some pointers about remaining in character. She couldn't believe Grace was flirting with strange men, men who could be sex traffickers and rapists. Grace knew how to work a room and every man in it. Zara was in awe, and it made what was going to happen that much more painful.

One evening, Grace and Zara were in a $10,000-a-hand private poker game. A man came in with a young girl who couldn't have been more than fifteen. Her makeup was done to make her look slightly older, but Grace knew that the girl's age was decades younger than the old man's. Grace had to mask her anger to get the job done.

She whispered to Zara, loud enough for the table to hear, "Isn't she cute? I want one of those." Zara nearly choked on her drink. She watched Grace as she licked her lips and addressed the man directly, "Where did an old man like you get a cutie like that? Even with money."

The old man sneered at Grace but ignored her. Grace didn't press it, but she could tell he was irritated. She turned to Zara and whispered in her ear, looking at the man and laughing as she did so. Grace told Zara to laugh. The dealer began to look nervous and the tension in the room grew. The older gentleman directed his companion to sit in a chair on the wall behind him.

Grace teased him. She purred, "Now, why did you put away the scenery?"

The other players looked between Grace and the old man to see if the banter would continue. Grace pulled back, playing the game with ease. Zara folded out as instructed after losing 50K, but she stayed, watching the game. She watched Grace outplay most of the players like she did this every day. Zara hoped she would ever be able to be as poised under pressure like this. Grace played a smart game, and the final hand of the night came down to her and the old man—just as she thought it would. The pot was up to $700K.

Grace's hole cards were a Nine and Ten of Diamonds. She knew she was about to risk a great deal, but she had to win. Inwardly, she groaned, hoping that he would be forced to fold. The dealer set the flop. A Jack of Diamonds, a King of Spades, and an Eight of Diamonds. She looked at her opponent. She saw the same sneer that meant he was about to call and raise the bet. He was too arrogant to know that he'd given away his tells all night. So, she decided to make it interesting.

"Call. Raise." The old man threw $100K worth of chips on the table. Grace wanted to smack the look off his face. She stared back at him.

The dealer set the Turn. A Queen of Diamonds.

Grace wanted to shout. The only way he could beat her now was if he was sitting on a Royal Flush. She held her breath as the dealer set the River. A King of Clubs. Grace looked at her opponent. He was salivating. He wiped his mouth, and with a gleam in his eye, looked at Grace and said, "I raise you $300K, and if you win, I'll let you borrow her for the night. I can always get another."

The dealer said nothing. No one said anything.

Grace looked around and then said to him, "And if I lose?"

"Then, I get you and that smart mouth of yours. And believe me, I know how to shut it up."

Without blinking an eye and never breaking eye contact, Grace shoved her chips forward. "All in." The pot was up to $1.2 million, and Grace knew she was playing a dangerous game.

The dealer finally spoke up. "Players, show your cards."

The old man, smiling, turned over four Kings and smugly said, "Four of a Kind," He sat back in his chair clearly satisfied with himself. He called the girl over to stand by him. Grace shrugged her shoulders.

"Good game, sir, but mine is better." Grace revealed her Straight Flush. She kept her eyes on her opponent but spoke to the dealer. "Please have my winnings delivered to my room." Grace paused for effect, "Well, not all of it. Come here, dear, you're mine for the evening." She motioned for Zara to head to the door. She walked around the table and took the girl's hand as the old man watched. His face was getting redder by the second. "I promise to take really good care of her." The old man tried to stop her, but he had to save face in front the other gamblers. A bet was a bet.

The girl made no protest, and Grace knew that she didn't believe that she even had a choice. Grace continued the charade all the way back to the hotel room. Grace and Zara flanked her in silence. When Zara opened the door to the suite, she waited until Grace spoke to say anything. Zara didn't know how far Grace would go in the game.

Grace was still in character as she asked the young girl her name. "What's your name sweetheart?"

The girl stood silent before them, her eyes darting from one to the others.

"You do have a name? And please sit, my dear." Grace motioned for her to sit on the sofa. Zara moved to sit directly across from the girl, poised, aloof, and on guard.

Finally, the girl spoke, "Katerina."

Grace continued, moving about the room as if this were the most natural conversation in the world. Zara watched the exchange like she was watching a movie. Grace floated around talking, seemingly absently, but asking pointed questions that Zara knew were for information. In no time, Grace had Katerina talking about herself and revealing more than she had intended. Katerina was fifteen, and she'd just met the old man that evening, introduced by a friend. Grace and Sara exchanged glances and knew that meant she had a pimp.

Grace dropped her accent, walked over to Katerina, and sat next to her on the sofa. "Do you want out of the life? Yes, or no?"

Katerina looked at Grace. Tears were brimming in Katerina's eyes as she looked at Grace. With barely a whisper, Katerina said "yes." The admission unleashed a torrent of tears, and Grace was able to hold her and let her cry.

Grace was rocking Katerina while issuing directives to Zara. "Call 555-438-4663. It's the Get-Home number of the State Department. We can call that number, and they'll dispatch an agent in the area."

Grace pulled Katerina up and walked her into the bedroom to take a shower and rest. She gave her some sweats and a t-shirt to wear. Grace could tell that the child was exhausted, mentally and physically. What horrors she'd been through, Grace could only imagine, but no matter what happened with the operation, she, at least, knew that someone had been spared.

As Zara watched the entire scene with Grace and Katerina unfold before her, she was overcome with shame. Grace truly cared about the work she was doing, and here she was about to betray her and the job. Zara walked to the suite's kitchenette to get a bottle of water. The movement kept her from running in the bedroom and telling Grace what she'd done and for whom. She had to save her family, just like this girl needed to be reunited with hers. Just thinking about it all, Zara felt the tears brimming her eyes. She wiped her face just as Grace reentered the room.

Grace noted the strange look on Zara's face. "Zara, are you okay? I know you weren't expecting this." Grace glanced at the bedroom and shrugged, "Neither was I."

Zara recovered and said, "I knew the nature of the job, but to see a victim..."

Grace cut her off, "A survivor."

Zara remembering how Grace always admonished them to see the girls and women as survivors rather than victims. "Right. To see a survivor so closely. But you were amazing. How you played the old man, getting the girl out of there and the money! Do they let you keep any of the winnings?"

Grace laughed. "I wish. No, we will replenish the budget for the expense of the operation and set up a fund to help the girls in the raid, including Katerina. Gives them a fresh start. No sense in saving someone from slavery if you can't give them a real start. It's not 40 acres and a mule, but it's something."

The knock at the door startled them both. Grace pulled her service revolver from her back and approached the door.

In her Parminder voice, she asked, "Who is it?"

The male voice on the other side of the door said, "Sauveur." Grace relaxed but motioned for Zara to cover the door. She opened it cautiously. An officer in his early thirties wearing black jeans and a black t-shirt that showed a chiseled chest and well-developed biceps appeared. "Chief sent me. You called the hotline."

"I.D.?" Zara's hand was still on her service revolver, and she was waiting on Grace's word to relax her hold.

The agent gave Grace his identification and badge with a smirk. "Chief said you would still ask."

After reviewing his credentials, Grace chuckled. "He knows me well. Come in, Agent King."

Agent King stepped into the suite and looked around the room. "Nice. Very nice." His eyes settled on Zara, and he gave her a nod. He whispered to Grace, "Is this the survivor?"

Grace shook her head. "No, the survivor's resting in the bedroom. I told her someone would be here soon. I'll get her."

While she went to get Katerina, Zara and Agent King engaged in small talk. After a few minutes, Grace and Katerina emerged from the bedroom, looking every bit the fifteen-year-old she was, no evidence of the heavy makeup and fake eyelashes. Grace introduced her to Agent King and hugged her. She whispered in her ear, "You're going to have a good life, Katerina." Releasing her from a hug, Grace said, "Agent King will be taking you to a safe house, and there will be someone there to help you navigate your next steps. You have my number. Okay?"

Katerina nodded. And looked at Agent King. "I'm ready."

Agent King looked at Grace and Katerina. "As a kid she can be in the casino restaurants, but not the floor. That will work to our advantage since there's a separate entrance to the restaurant. You'll get a signal call when she's out of harm's way."

"Thank you, Agent King."

Grace closed the door and leaned against it. She looked at Zara, who looked as tired as she felt. "Get some rest, Zara. It's showtime tomorrow."

CHAPTER 14

Kenzo couldn't sleep. He tried to focus on some paperwork for a new building he and Riley were thinking of acquiring for development, but something was haunting him. He knew Grace could handle herself, but the thought that his woman was being sabotaged meant that she was vulnerable. Kenzo was restless, and for the first time, he couldn't lose himself in work. He walked aimlessly around the house, opening and closing the refrigerator, cleaning up imaginary messes in his mind. Finally, he settled on a glass of Malbec and a dose of Miles. This was a Miles kind of night. He sat there through "Round Midnight" and "So What" with his eyes closed, absorbing the sound and talking himself out of driving to the Coast. Before he knew it, he'd drifted into prayer.

"Lord, protect her. And help me, I can't lose her. You sent her to me. Don't take her now. Please."

Kenzo took in a deep breath and sat on the sofa with his eyes closed. Grace's face came to him, her smiling face, the bliss in her face when she ate something delicious, the way she cocked her head to the left when she was thinking, and then, the look on her face the first time he'd told her he loved her.

Kenzo opened his eyes and reached for his phone. Marcus was supposed to call him, but he hadn't. For some reason, though, he wasn't as worried, but he knew he needed to be there. Something was going to happen, of that he was sure, but he wouldn't interfere unless someone forced his hand. He dialed Marcus's number and walked to his bedroom to pack. Marcus picked up on the third ring.

Marcus didn't say hello but just starting talking. "Man, you must be reading my mind. I just got some intel that you need to see."

Kenzo stopped in his tracks. "Where are you? I'll meet you."

"No need, brother. I'll be at your place in ten minutes."

Kenzo heard the line click. And for a moment, he was frozen in place. If Marcus was coming to see him personally, then this was serious. He jolted himself into action. He wanted to have his bag at the door so that he would be ready to leave as soon as Marcus finished. In record time, Kenzo threw his clothes and toiletries in a bag and was waiting for Marcus when he drove up. He opened the door before Marcus could even knock.

"What you got, man?" Kenzo's attempt to maintain cool was lost the moment he saw the haggard look on Marcus's face.

Marcus walked in talking. Well, I think I found the weak link, but I want you to see it all."

"Marcus, my woman can't be down there on a 'think."

"Listen, I had to call in every contact and favor I had to get folks to call in favors from their contacts. I didn't realize Grace was that bad. Man, and I do mean baaaaad."

Kenzo couldn't help but smile at Marcus. "I know, man."

"Well, I had to access her records from the State Department and every case she's had. There's one case that kept coming back to me. And I think that's the start. Grace's first lead was to infiltrate a ring in Paris. When the cops moved in, the perp's son was just twelve. And he was there. And get this, the boy's mother was her husband's right hand. Like the trafficking was a family business."

"What does this have to do with Grace's current case?" Marcus was always long-winded.

"Flight records show that the mother landed at Jackson-Evers two months ago." He looked at Kenzo and said, "I don't know about you, but if I live in Paris, I don't take vacations in Jackson, Mississippi."

Kenzo nodded. "True. Was she seen with anyone?"

"Yes, bank records show that she checked into a hotel in downtown Jackson. She *was only here for two days and then she rented a car and went to the Coast."*

"What about her team? Grace thinks it might be the young one, Edward."

"He's clean. Terry's clean. Luther's clean. But get this, you know the girl, Zara?

"Yeah, Grace has mentioned her. She considers Zara her protégé."

"Her father's been damn near living in Vicksburg at the sports betting bar, and her mother's got at least $100,000 in medical bills. The medical bills were enough, but the father's bookie is Shotgun."

"You've got to be kidding me. Who in the hell would still bet with Shotgun?" Shotgun was notorious. Kenzo, Marcus, and Riley all went to school with Shotgun when she was just Shay. But, at sixteen, Shay's mother was murdered by her father, and she was left responsible for her siblings and a sick grandmother. Shotgun did whatever she had to do. She started working the streets and selling dope, but soon graduated to murder, gambling, and hits. She had men working for her twice her age, sometimes three, who wouldn't cross her.

Marcus pulled out a photograph of Zara's father. "This fool. And he owed Shotgun big money. Until yesterday. Half of his debt was paid—fifty stacks."

"That's all I need to hear. I'm out." Kenzo grabbed his keys. "I'll call RIley from the car. Y'all meet me down there. I've got to get word to Grace who she's dealing with."

Kenzo called Riley and gave him a run-down of the situation. He and Marcus were going to follow him within the hour. And then he made one final phone call.

To Shotgun.

Kenzo pulled into Smith Park and waited. Shotgun arrived shortly after he did, and they both emerged from their respective cars and stood across from each other. Her number two man stayed in the car. After a second or two, Shotgun spoke, "Man, you got real problems if you're calling me out like this."

Kenzo looked at his old friend. Shay, or Shotgun, had a hard life, but few knew that they were friends who had gone to school together. When the kids bullied her for not having new clothes or shoes, Kenzo defended her, even got suspended once for fighting on her behalf. But they had always been friends. When her mother died, his family went to the funeral and helped out as much as they could.

After a while, Kenzo and Shay lost touch, and Shay became Shotgun while he was still trying to figure out who he was. Shotgun got the name for obvious reasons. She carried a double-barreled stage coach shotgun on her hip and was quick to use it. She'd taken out most of her enemies and set up her own enterprise by age twenty-one. Shotgun was now stacked and gorgeous, not that gangly little girl he met in the fifth grade. She used her beauty to her advantage, to distract and disarm, but she wasn't afraid to make an example of anyone. Even now, the black cat suit she wore was flanked by a nine-millimeter. She had her hand in most of the criminal activity in Jackson and had opened up legitimate businesses to clean her money from nightclubs to laundromats. Kenzo could never work with her if he was to keep his business clean, but he couldn't help but admire the hustle. She put all of her siblings through college and forbade them to return to Jackson. She never wanted them to see her as Shotgun, just Shay.

"Yeah. The name Lawrence Bailey mean anything to you?"

Shotgun raised her eyebrow. "Yes. Why?"

"Heard he owed you money."

"What of it? Lots of folks owe me, but they don't owe me long. And you know we have a rule, Kenzo. We don't talk about business. You're straight. I'm not. That's not going to change."

"His debt was paid by someone looking to take out my woman. His daughter may be a dirty cop."

"Damn. Lawrence Bailey is a degenerate gambler, man. I'm not surprised. Glad you're dating again though. Was getting really worried about you."

"Thanks." Kenzo nodded toward the man watching him from the car. "He cool? Looks like he's ready to shoot."

Shotgun laughed. "Yeah, he's cool. He better be. I don't do questions." She looked back at her car and back at Kenzo, "So what's up?"

Kenzo turned his attention back to Shotgun. "I'm headed to the Coast. Something's going down, and I have a feeling that Bailey is involved. I need some heavy artillery, and I may need some backup."

"You know, I got you. I'll call my boys on the Coast. Some bad guys who can handle bad things. You just let me know. I'll put them on standby."

"Cool. Thanks, Shay."

"You still the only person who can call me that and get away with it."

"I won't tell if you don't." Kenzo got back in his car and peeled out of the parking lot. He hoped like hell he wouldn't have to call in Shotgun even though deep down he knew he would. He didn't know how he would be able to explain Shotgun, the criminal, to Grace, the cop. *Jesus*, Kenzo thought. Hopefully, he wouldn't have to...at least not yet.

Kenzo checked into a hotel, having called and made reservations along the way. His efforts to reach Grace failed. Her phone kept going straight to voicemail, which meant it was either completely turned off or something had happened. Either way was unacceptable at this point. Frustrated, he threw the phone on the seat beside him. He was determined not to be *that guy*, which is why when she didn't offer the details, he didn't ask.

Marcus and Riley arrived shortly after he did. The hardest thing for Kenzo was not knowing where she was. Marcus was having a hard time finding her. The Coast was small enough to feel like home and big enough to get lost in. With three large cities and small towns all on the coastline, Kenzo wouldn't have known where to look, so he had to look everywhere. He didn't know where she was or any details, but Marcus's contacts had said that the chatter on the Darknet was that a flesh auction was taking place the next day. The three of them spent the better part of the night trying to figure out how to be near the action without interfering in Grace's operation. But every moment that he didn't know where Grace was meant that she was in danger. She needed to know about Zara before something happened.

If he or Riley showed up at any part of this, Kenzo knew that even the slightest recognition would throw her off. Marcus was the only one she didn't know, and he'd be there, wired, so Kenzo and Riley could listen from their car. It was all too James Bond for him, but Kenzo had no choice. If the bust went down as planned, they went home. If it didn't, he'd be there.

The details of the location of the auction were kept secret until just before. Marcus would be the one getting the information and would use one of his aliases to gain entry. Until then, they waited.

The morning of every operation started the same. Grace got up at 5:00 a.m. for a run to clear her head, a large breakfast of whatever decadence she wanted, including French toast. Especially French toast. Then, a hot shower and a good long nap. She was feeling good after last night's impromptu rescue. She got a call the moment the girl was in a safe house and her parents notified. Grace considered it a good omen for tonight.

Grace drove to her dummy hotel that morning and took a run on the beach. A good run got her blood pumping, and by the time she'd run five miles, she was ravenous. The restaurant next door to the hotel was still serving breakfast, and she took her time, enjoying the view, watching couples and children play along the beach. She allowed herself to imagine herself and Kenzo walking along the beach holding hands, and then, she had a vision of him running behind a little boy and girl. *Where in the world did that come from?* But it was a nice reverie if only for a few moments. She got up and her eyes met those of a gentleman who was enjoying his breakfast alone as well. She smiled and said, "good morning", paid her bill, and left.

The man watched her leave and pulled out his phone. "I found her."

Zara was still asleep when she returned. Everyone had their rituals, she supposed. She moved about the suite as quietly as possible before retiring to her room for a nap. As she showered, she went over the details of the evening. As soon as they received the instructions, they would have an hour to get in place. Edward and Terry would inform them as soon as the word came. And she knew that Chief and his team would as well. Since Grace was the only one aware of the shadow team, she was confident that whoever the mole was in her camp would be apprehended right along with the traffickers. For now, she simply had to watch everyone and prepare herself for the fallout.

Just as she was settling down for her nap, the phone rang. She was loathed to answer it, but she was glad she hadn't yet drifted off to sleep. That would have been ugly. Using her accent, Grace answered the phone, clearly irritated. At least that part was all Grace and not Parminder.

116

Kenzo hesitated, but he heard Grace's spirit beneath the accent. He kept his message short and sweet. "Back stairwell, 12th floor. Five minutes." He hung up the house phone in the lobby and casually shoved his hands in the pockets of his jeans. Just hearing her voice, knowing she was so close to him, had his heart thumping in his chest. He measured his steps so as to not draw suspicion as he walked to the elevator bank. He rode to the eleventh floor and headed toward the stairwell. He got there before she did and paced back and forth to calm his nerves. When the door opened, Kenzo turned to see a very angry Grace Harrington ready to lay into him.

Through gritted teeth, Grace exclaimed, "Kenzo, what are you doing here!? You cannot be here. This is dangerous and you're putting my whole operation at jeopardy!" She couldn't believe he'd showed up here and put so much at risk. She was too angry to acknowledge the desire burning within her at the very sight of him. She crossed her arms and glared at him, waiting for his explanation for this gross violation.

While her eyes were angry and questioning, Kenzo zeroed in on the sexy pout of her lips. Grace was so angry that she didn't realize that he was closing in on her. Before she knew it, Kenzo had her face in her hands and had slammed his mouth on hers. He was devouring her mouth like a starving man, and God help her, Grace found herself giving him as good as he was giving. After a few moments, Kenzo broke the kiss, placing his forehead on hers as his breathing normalized. He held her close, needing to inhale her scent, to feel her nearness. His arms were the only place that he knew, for sure, was safe. Grace extricated herself and without a word, demanded an explanation.

Kenzo looked at her square. Seeing her made him almost forget why he was here. "It's Zara."

Grace thought she misheard him. "What? What are you saying?"

"Zara is your mole, baby. Her father owed gambling debts that were off the books."

Grace narrowed her eyes at Kenzo. "How would you know this? Where did you get your information?"

Kenzo saw Grace go full cop in five seconds and was impressed. "Right now, I got the info from an old friend, and I didn't want you going in there blind. I'll tell you how I got it later. Trust me. She's dirty."

Grace felt like the wind had been knocked out of her. She'd suspected Edward, maybe even Terry, but not Zara. But she knew Kenzo wouldn't have come if he wasn't sure. She walked to the opposite corner of the stairwell. Her mind was racing. She had to go through with the operation, and for some reason, she believed Kenzo. No one else, including Chief, had been able to find anything. How he was able to she wasn't quite sure she wanted to know.

Kenzo watched the wheels in her head spin. "What do you want to do?"

"Well, I can't very well nix the operation. Too much is at stake and we're too close. Chief told me that I was a target and its was personal, from one of my first cases."

Kenzo shouted before he could stop himself, "Why in the hell didn't you cancel this shit then? You were going to do it anyway knowing that!"

Grace hissed back, "Keep your voice down. Yes, this is what I do, and I don't run because there's a threat to my life. Chief is running a shadow team that my team doesn't know about, so I could flush out the plant."

"Well, I'm telling you the plant is Zara. So now what?" Kenzo was growing increasingly frustrated and his voice was agitated. Grace had intentionally used herself as bait, which could have been disastrous if things had gone wrong. But now wasn't the time to go caveman on Grace. Demanding that she pull out of this wasn't going to work for her at all. *Regroup, man,* he told himself. Kenzo eased toward Grace tentatively, like he was approaching a wounded animal. He placed his hands on her shoulders, grounding them both. "What do you need from me? What can I do to help you? Just don't ask me to leave. Don't ask me to let you go into the Lion's Den without me."

Grace looked at Kenzo. She knew how difficult this was for him. Taking the risks she did never bothered Jaden, and she never thought about him. It was the job. "Listen, we don't have the details yet. The call will come in a few hours. If Zara is compromised..."

Kenzo interrupted her, "She is."

Grace took in a breath and continued in a stern tone, "If Zara is compromised, I'll alert Chief, so he can put a man on her when the takedown happens."

"What are you going to do until then?" Kenzo really didn't want her going back into that suite with someone who wanted to harm her.

"Until then, I wait and watch. When I left, she was still asleep, so she doesn't even know I came back, which works in my favor. I'll go back in and be on guard until showtime."

Kenzo thought that was a bit too loose for him. "Will you, at least, turn your phone on and call me when everything pops off?"

Grace knew that would be a bad idea, but she knew that he would not be deterred. She agreed and hoped he would keep his distance. "But, Kenzo, you have to promise me that you'll stay away. This is what I do."

Begrudgingly, Kenzo agreed to keep his distance, but both Grace and Kenzo knew that there was no way in hell that he was staying away.

"Please, Kenzo."

He kissed her on her forehead and whispered. "Go on back to your room, Love." When she looked up at him, he saw the love in her eyes. He hoped she saw love in his. Kenzo bent to kiss her one more time. He kissed her with every emotion he had—love, passion, anger, and fear. He wanted it to fuel her, not distract her. He needed her to know that there was someone waiting for her, that he would be waiting for her.

CHAPTER 15

The call had come. Participants would go to what looked like an abandoned warehouse and give go through several layers of security checks to ensure that they weren't wired or carrying weapons. Luckily, Grace had access to state-of-the-art technology that was so next-level that it hadn't been used in many operations. The microphones were undetectable and woven into the fibers of their clothes. Their firearms were covered with a polymer and wouldn't be detect by metal detectors. Grace had also been working with a 3D Glock since it seemed that criminals were getting just as paranoid as law enforcement. Grace worried whether Zara had compromised everything, and she wouldn't know until it was too late if she had. These people would kill on the spot and walk over your body while it was still warm.

Grace watched Zara fidget and pace in the last hour. Where she once chalked it up to first-time nerves, she now believed it was more. As far as Grace was concerned, Zara was under suspicion, and Grace needed to treat her that way. Grace scrutinized every detail she remembered about Zara's family. Grace played their conversations overin her head, realizing that when they did talk about family, Zara focused more on her mother's battle with cancer. Zara never talked about her father. As they waited, Grace thought it best to find out more about the protégé she thought she knew. Zara was clearly nervous; she was double checking everything. Before her visit from Kenzo, Grace would have been amused, but now she saw much more in the action and decided to use it to her advantage.

"Zara, why don't you have a seat? You're working yourself up. Anxiety isn't good for an operation like this."

Zara stopped and looked at Grace. Grace had been nothing but kind to her from the beginning. She mentored her, listened to her. And even now, Grace was being kind. She wasn't angry about Zara's nervousness, just concerned. It made Zara sick, knowing that a woman she admired would be dead soon because her father couldn't stop gambling. He didn't know what he cost their family, what he was costing her. "I'm sorry. Just nervous. I want to make sure that I'm prepared. I don't want to disappoint you." Zara had to look away as she said the last part, as she knew she already had, even if Grace didn't know it.

"You'll be fine. You've trained for this, right?"

"Yes. But..."

"But, nothing. These sharks smell fear. If you go in there with any doubt, then the game is over. Understand?"

"Yes, I know you're right. But I..."

"While we wait, let's talk about something else. How's your mom?"

Zara wanted to vomit. "She's responding well to chemo and the doctors are hoping that the tumor shrinks enough before surgery to remove it all."

"And your father?" Grace asked nonchalantly. "How is he handling your mother's illness?"

"Not well. But then, he never was good at handling most things. Mama always referred to him as her 'bonus child'." Zara's sarcastic laugh was not lost on Grace. Yep, the father was a problem.

"Most men are. I know my father can run an entire platoon and a base, but my mother could never get him to do anything around the house. It drives her crazy." Grace laughed because it was true. Her father was so used to giving orders and having menial tasks handled at work, he couldn't bring himself to do them at home.

Zara smiled a weak smile at Grace and fingered the ring on her hand. She turned the ring toward her palm, but it was beginning to feel tight and constraining against her skin.

Grace noticed the ring for the first time since Zara was fidgeting with it so.

"That's a beautiful piece. May I see it?"

Zara looked down at the ring that had become like an albatross around her neck. She held out her hand for Grace. The ring sparkled in the light, and Zara couldn't help but acknowledge the irony, even if it was just to herself.

Grace held her hand firmly as she pretended to "ooh" and "ahh" over the ring. "Gift? Heirloom?" Grace kept her voice as light as she could. She wanted to ask her outright, but she knew that for the long haul, she needed to catch her, make the connections. What worried her was how deep Zara was covered, and how in the hell Kenzo could get information when Chief couldn't. She noticed the sadness in Zara's eyes as she responded, "Heirloom. From my father's side." The lie was a technicality, but one that Zara couldn't deny. All her father had ever given her mother and her was grief.

Just as Grace was about to ask her more questions, her cell phone rang. It was Terry with the details about where and when. Grace joked with Zara one final time. "Last bathroom break." As Zara moved into her en-suite bathroom, Grace watched Zara's slumped shoulders and the somberness of her gait. Until that moment, Grace had hoped Kenzo was wrong. Just as she was turning the corner, Zara looked back at Grace, who mustered a shy smile as she retreated to her own space for a last moment of peace and prayer.

Marcus had tapped into the hotel security systems and had an eye on the hallway of Grace's room. Kenzo wanted to know the moment Grace and Zara left the room. At the same time, he and Marcus had access to video feeds throughout the hotel from the front entrance to the back stairwell. Riley, refusing to watch empty hallways, was making sure that they had enough weapons.

As he loaded clips, Riley was chuckling, "Man, what I want to know is how are you going to explain Shotgun to your woman? Grace is sweet, but she carries a gun. After all this time of not having a woman, you pick a she-Rambo!"

Kenzo glared at Riley, saying nothing. Marcus was laughing so hard he had to wipe tears from his eyes as he begged Riley to stop talking.

"Hell if I will stop. Kenzo gon' get us all arrested, or worse." Pointing at Marcus and ignoring Kenzo's glare, Riley said, "You tapping into casino security. We sitting here with a damn arsenal, and best of all, Shotgun's crew is posted outside. We better hope Grace is in the frame of mind to save our asses if this gets ugly."

Kenzo was too focused on the screen to entertain Riley. Marcus was laughing at Riley when Grace and Zara's suite door opened.

"Here we go. They're on the move." Kenzo called Shotgun's head man downstairs. He'd already given him pictures of Grace and Zara so he could identify her and follow her car. Kenzo, Riley, and Marcus strapped up and headed for the stairwell. Kenzo had booked a room on the second floor so he would have to take the elevator. Good thing, too, since he might strangle Zara on the spot if he saw her. Marcus had both holsters but was carrying the laptop for the security feed, which meant Riley and Kenzo had to carry the remaining weapons.

As the trio descended the stairs, Marcus cursed. "Damn! Something's wrong."

Kenzo felt his blood go cold the moment his hand touched the door.

Marcus was tapping furiously. "The feed went out. The screens went black as if the cameras were disabled."

Kenzo burst through the door. He nearly toppled a hotel employee in the process and would have run out of there had Riley not caught his arm.

Riley whispered, "Steady, man, steady. We are three black men, with a bag full of guns. This is not the time to rouse attention or suspicion." Riley held Kenzo in place for a few seconds until he was sure what he said had registered.

Kenzo nodded and slowed his pace to a brisk gait. Kenzo didn't want to believe what he knew to be true. Grace was gone. He just prayed that Shotgun's men had an eye on whatever car she was in.

Two of Shotgun's men, Harp and LG, were watching from the hotel's back parking lot. When two shadowy figures exited from the back stairwell carrying a woman over their shoulders, Harp checked the pictures of Grace and Zara on his phone. The one walking was definitely Zara, so it didn't take long to figure out who the other one was. LG didn't talk much, but when he did, he was saying something profound. As Harp threw the car in gear to follow, LG mumbled, "I was hoping no one had to die tonight."

Harp chuckled in response, "Me too, brother, me too. Call the other guys and tell them we have an eyeball on the girls. I don't see Kenzo's crew, so call him too. Looks like they're heading east on I-10."

Minutes later, Harp followed the car to an abandoned building. He had three cars in his caravan. Harp and LG took the side of the parking lot closest to the car holding Grace. The others spread out in the parking lot while never taking their eyes off each other's cars. Harp placed the car in park and killed his lights. Kenzo wasn't far behind him. He saw Zara exit the car with three men. Harp could hear her crying and pleading with the men not to hurt Grace.

LG grunted as he leaned forward to get a better look at the scene.

Just then, Harp and LG watched as one of the men shot Zara at point blank range. She crumpled in a heap on the ground. The shooter turned to the third nameless man and pointed. Harp and LG couldn't hear what they were saying but it was soon clear that he was to take her body to the dumpster. They watched as Zara's lifeless body was literally hurled into the dumpster like trash.

LG shook his head, "Damn."

Grace lifted her head and looked around the dark room. Her hands were cuffed behind her. She was groggy, so she knew she'd been drugged. Grace tried to piece together the events that led her there. Grace remembered Zara opening the door to leave and entering the hallway behind her. Within a few steps toward the elevator, everything went black. *Where was Zara*, she asked herself. She realized that she still had her clothes on, so that was good. *Maybe she didn't tell them everything*, she thought. If her clothes were on, she was still wired, which means she had a record of what was happening.

Grace looked around the room. No windows. It was little more than a closet with a door. The only things she could do was wait and preserve her strength until then. She put her head back down and took in deep breaths. When her kidnappers returned, they needed to think she was still unaware of what was going on. Part of her wanted Zara to be with them. Zara needed to face her.

It didn't take long before she heard the door creak open. Someone turned on the lights. Grace listened to the different footsteps based on the soles. A male of average height and weight and a woman's heels. Stilettoes. She lifted her head, and though it was a little clearer, Grace continue to behave as if she were still drugged. She committed their faces to memory and hung her head again.

She heard a woman's voice first. "How much of that stuff did you give her? Is she going to be ready?"

Grace heard an accent. Must be Amir's mother. Her voice was mature enough to be. *But ready for what?* she wondered.

The man's voice was much younger, and she heard the deference in his voice. "I gave her the right amount. She's just a little groggy. I'll get some water for her. That will bring her around." Grace kept her head lowered as she heard the door close. A few minutes later, the man returned. He grabbed her roughly by her hair and threw the water in her face. Strangely satisfied with himself, he yanked her up, and though Grace could have overpowered him, she needed to see how far this was going. Plus, she had no weapon, so she had to be smart and play this to the bone. She had to remind herself that she'd trained for this. And whatever she had to do to survive, she would do.

In silence, he pulled her through dark hallways of a dilapidated building. She'd hoped that it was where the auction was being held, which meant she had backup somewhere. She memorized every detail she could despite the dull gray cement walls, mentally taking note of the number of steps and turns she was taking. She'd need the information if she got out of there. *When, Grace, when,* she reminded herself.

Her handler led her to another room. Another room with just a chair. *So, we're playing musical chairs, I see,* she thought. Roughly, he pushed her toward the chair, and placing a hand on her shoulder, pushed her down. This time her legs were bound as well. She said nothing but glared at him, which only amused her captor. When he left, she heard the lock click. Grace studied the room, wishing she could walk around the room, touch the walls for hidden compartments, and find anything that would help her. Finding nothing, she sat and waited for the next step.

Grace figured that about fifteen minutes had passed when the door opened. A beautiful woman in her late 40s stepped in the room. She was impeccably dressed in a black mini dress that Treasure would have killed to wear and wore spiked Louboutin heels. The woman stood squarely in front of her with a smirk on her face. The woman slowly circled Grace, her heels clicking against the hard floor. When the woman faced Grace again, she paused long enough for Grace to look at her. When their eyes met, the woman raised her hand and slapped her with the back of her hand. Grace saw the slap coming, so she turned her head to mitigate the effect of the blow, but it still hurt like hell. What hurt most was that she saw the glint from the rubies and diamonds in the ring on her right hand. It was the same ring that Zara wore.

Grace tasted her blood. "Ms. Amir Hassem, I presume. Beautiful ring. A friend of mine has one just like it." Grace was trying to maintain her calm façade even though she was seething on the inside.

The woman hit her again, this time with an open palm. "It's Mrs. I am Mrs. Anika Hassem." She said it proudly and with emphasis. "And you will pay for taking him from me, from our son," she hissed. She looked down at her ring. "Yes, I'm sure you have. It's a family ring of sorts."

Grace smiled as she licked the blood from the corner of her mouth. "I'm sure. your husband got just what he deserved. As will you. And so will anyone else..." she said as she spat blood on the floor, "in your family."

"You will know what it feels like to be humiliated in front of all you hold dear. And my son will deal with you as his father should have." She rolled her shoulders to compose herself and smoothed invisible wrinkles with her hands. "Yes, I'm going to enjoy this much more than I thought I would."

Edward, Luther, and Terry exchanged looks in the car. Neither Grace, nor Zara were answering, which meant that something was wrong. But Grace had prepared them for the scenario if they needed to fall back. Terry, as the senior officer, was to continue the ruse and take as much intel as possible. Just as they were exiting their car, a black Mercedes came to a screeching halt beside them. Kenzo jumped out with such panic that Edward nearly pulled his gun.

Terry recognized him before shots were fired, "Kenzo, what in the holy hell are you doing here?"

Kenzo felt his heart pounding in his chest. "I had some information to give Grace. Zara compromised your entire operation, man! And they grabbed Grace just as they were leaving the hotel."

Edward broke in, "Zara? You've got to be kidding. She's a good cop." Ignoring Kenzo and turning to Terry and Luther, "C'mon, y'all, we need to get to work."

Kenzo wanted to break his face. Through gritted teeth, he said, "Listen, I don't have time for this. They have Grace somewhere in this building. My man, Marcus, is getting the specs for the building. But I need to get into that building."

Terry felt in his gut that something was wrong and that worried him. Good cops always listened to their gut. He turned to Edward and Luther. You stay here. I'm going to take Kenzo in with me." Before Edward could protest, he continued. "You get the building specs and work the perimeter with..." He looked at Kenzo to complete the sentence. Luther understood. The way things were going, he'd much rather be outside. The building looked like a tomb, and he wasn't ready to die.

"Marcus and Riley. And don't ask, but we're strapped."

Terry nodded. "I'm sure you are, but you can't take anything in there. They're checking everyone."

Kenzo was prepared for that. "They're not checking where my piece is. Let's go." Kenzo turned to Riley, who by now had gotten out of the car. "When Marcus gets the specs, get Shotgun's boys on the perimeter. Do what you have to do."

Edward piped up, "Hey, I'm in charge." As if he'd just remembered Luther standing beside him, "I mean we're in charge."

Luther shook his head and smiled dryly at him. Luther outranked Edward by so many years that if he wanted to, he could have embarrassed him on the spot. Edward could barely be in control of himself.

Kenzo stared at Edward as if he'd forgotten he was there. "Yeah, okay."

———

Terry and Kenzo approached the steel door. A sliding window opened, and two eyes gave them a once over and opened the door. The large man guarding the door, in a gruff voice said, "Password."

Terry said in a clear voice, "Amour à vendre." Kenzo fought not to roll his eyes.

They were then ushered into a large room. A makeshift stage had been constructed and a row of computers were set up facing the stage in numbered stations. Terry and Kenzo were ushered to Stations 5 and 6, dead center of the stage. The stations were set up around the room in a large oval. Each station had a light that was either green or red depending on your bid. The light remained red until the bidder became the highest bidder. Then, the light stayed green.

Other men and women were in place at stations. Kenzo looked around trying to figure out the process. Terry sensed his confusion and whispered to him, "Welcome to a 21st century slave auction. If you see a girl you want, you have to bid in cryptocurrency. It's untraceable."

Scantily clad girls and women were walking around with trays of food and drinks. Terry and Kenzo each took a drink but knew not to take a sip. Terry slipped Kenzo Edward's password. "Log in with Edward's information. You'll need to make bids at first, but the plan has changed. If they have Grace, and Zara has done what you said she did, then they know who we are. At least, they know me."

Kenzo watched a man enter the room from the back. He noted that the door was one of those that blended into the wall so that you had to know where it was to access it. It was as if he simply appeared in the room. The man surveyed the collection of men as they prepared themselves for the night's event. When his eyes landed on Kenzo and Terry, the man paused long enough to assess them, but not long enough to be noticeable.

Kenzo whispered to Terry, "I think we've been made, but let's see where this goes. They could have killed us already."

Terry let out a sigh. "Yep."

Everyone was taking their seats, so Kenzo and Terry did the same. A second later, the lights went black and a spotlight shone in the middle of the stage. Kenzo held his breath. *Lord, help me,* Kenzo prayed. The well-dressed man walked to the spotlight and explained the rules. All transactions would be in cryptocurrency through the Darknet portal already on the screens. Winning bids will be satisfied at the close of the auction.

Kenzo watched as girl after girl was led to the spotlight, and he grew more disgusted as the night progressed. Their ages ranged from thirteen to twenty, each wearing lingerie and heels. Some didn't look like they were out of middle school, while others were trussed up to appear older. Some stumbled in the heels, unused to them, but they all looked dazed as they turned in a circle. A woman's voice described each girl as if she was in a fashion show, highlighting their attributes from whether they were fluent in different languages, their ages, and any other skills that would make them attractive to bidders. It was nothing more than a slave auction, and Kenzo remembered his first night at dinner with Grace and the tears in her eyes when she talked about her work. Now, he completely understood. It was sickening. Six figure bids were announced after each girl was bought. A little girl was sold for $300,000. She looked like she was playing dress-up in her mother's clothes. Just as Kenzo wanted to go Rambo, the woman began speaking.

"Last but not least, gentlemen, we have a special treat tonight."

Kenzo didn't think he could take another virgin-child on the stage. He closed his eyes, but the woman continued.

"She speaks three languages—English, French, and Arabic...".

Kenzo's eyes popped open. Grace was standing in the spotlight. Unlike the others, she was dressed in what Kenzo assumed was the pantsuit she was wearing when they snatched her. He and Grace's eyes met, and she remained stoic, except for the plea he saw in her eyes.

From a remote place in his mind, he heard the announcer's voice. "Would you like to see more gentlemen?"

A chorus of affirmative grunts bounced off the walls. The house lights came up. No one was hidden. Anika wanted her to see their faces. Unlike the others who could hide under the spotlight because they couldn't see the faces of those who sought to abuse them, Grace was forced to see the men and women who peddled in stolen souls.

The man stood in front of her and ripped open her jacket, sending the buttons flying and revealing her bra. The buttons pinged on the cement floor. It was then that Kenzo noticed that her hands were cuffed. He knew his woman. If he could get them to uncuff her, then she could defend herself.

Grace refused to cry when she saw Kenzo. When they ripped open her jacket, she saw the anger rise in him. But she couldn't get her hands free.

A man's voice in the darkness called out. "Can we see her without the jacket? And the pants. Like the others."

"Most certainly, sir. We want all to have the complete experience. We will start the bidding at $100,000."

Grace couldn't wait to slap her face. Hard.

Amir and his mother were enjoying their victory too early. They never should have brought her here, in this room. She saw Chief out of the corner of her eye. She knew she had backup. Two sets. More than enough.

The man who walked her to the stage moved behind her and uncuffed her. As he was pulling her jacket from her shoulders, she reached behind her and pulled her 9mm glock from the bra strap. In a blur, she turned around and kicked him, knocking him against the wall. Grace spied one of Hassem's henchmen reach for his weapon in his coat and pointed her gun at him. She worried about the bullet ricocheting and hitting innocents and even the guilty, so she had to make it a clean kill shot. Grace yelled, "Gun!" and pulled the trigger, hitting the henchman dead center of his forehead.

As soon as the shot rang out, all guns in the room were drawn. Grace was breathing hard, her adrenaline pumping. She was trying to determine the good guys from the bad, but she couldn't beyond the faces she knew—Chief, Terry, and Kenzo. She didn't know all of Chief's crew, but she knew he had at least two in the room.

All of sudden, chaos ensued. As if on cue, the building was ambushed. Both entrances into the room burst open and guns were drawn from all sides. Gunfire rang out, and she dodged a bullet from one of Hassem's goons. She didn't get a chance to fire one back before he was hit. Someone flipped on all the house lights, and there was an armed man at every station within seconds. She only knew a handful of people, but she had a sneaky suspicion that Kenzo had something to do with the heavy artillery and extra manpower.

With razor focus, Grace could see the entire room, including the upstairs viewing room. Amir and Anika had been there watching and emceeing the auction, but Luther and Edward caught them at a back stairwell that Marcus found in the plans. She saw Edward and Luther enter the room with Amir and his mother in handcuffs.

Chief, Terry, Luther, and Chief's people were handcuffing the bidders and the Hassems' remaining henchmen. Edward had called local law enforcement to transport the bidders to the jails and escort the rescued girls to safety.

Grace turned around in a circle. Everyone was here but one. She looked between Edward and Terry. "Where is Zara?"

Chief and Terry said they didn't know yet, but Edward spoke up. "She's dead. They must have killed her the moment they nabbed you. We found her in a dumpster. They just dumped her like she was trash."

Grace felt like she'd been kicked in the gut. Despite her betrayals, she didn't deserve to die like that. Grace walked over to Amir and his mother. She wanted to put a bullet in them both. She was storming in their direction when she felt Kenzo's hand on her arms.

"Grace, don't do it." His voice was soft, almost hypnotic.

Grace's rage was fueling her adrenaline, but the warmth of Kenzo's touch and the silkiness of his voice stopped her. He handed her the jacket that had been thrown to the floor. In all of what was going on, Grace forgot that she was walking around in her bra. Kenzo almost looked sheepish, because as much as he didn't want her embarrassed, he saw how many men were taking a few sidelong glances, lingering a few seconds too long.

Grace silently mouthed, "Thank you" to Kenzo, but then turned her attentions to the Hassems. Looking at them, she called for Edward. "Edward, get this trash out of here."

Anika Hassem spit at Grace as officers led them out. She spewed curses at Grace and vowed revenge.

Amir Hassem said nothing. Grace almost felt sorry for him. His life was ruined because his mother was fueled by revenge and hatred. He was just as abused, having to grow up under that kind of vitriol and criminal legacy.

Grace was holding her jacket closed as she oversaw the arrests and confiscation of the computers and every scrap of paper. The additional men, all of whom Grace was sure were criminals themselves, had been allowed to leave. She made a mental note to ask Kenzo about it later, but right now, she needed to wash this day off.

Kenzo posted himself against the door, never taking his eyes off her, as she worked. He was in awe of Grace and the way she took control of the crime scene while simultaneously ensuring that the girls had what they need. The only time he saw her falter was when she met with the coroner to identify Zara's body. Kenzo wanted to reach out to her, but he knew that she couldn't demonstrate any vulnerability on the job. He tried to blend into the background, so he wouldn't distract her or call her leadership into question.

She left Terry in charge of the collection of evidence, and she turned to Kenzo, who was waiting patiently by the door. As professionally as she could, she said, "Mr. Dallas. Would you mind giving me a lift to my hotel?"

Kenzo pushed off the wall. "Yes, ma'am. I don't mind."

Grace nodded, reminding Terry to secure the evidence and they would meet at 9:00 a.m. sharp to prepare for her meeting with the federal prosecutor. She walked out without a backward glance, and Kenzo followed behind her like the chauffeur he was all too happy to be.

As soon as they were outside, Kenzo surveyed the empty parking lot. He grabbed Grace's arm and turned her around. He pulled her to him and slammed his mouth on hers. Kenzo couldn't help himself. He needed to taste her, to feel her in his arms. She opened her mouth for him, and Kenzo devoured her mouth, finding her tongue, nibbling on her lips, licking and sucking them as if they were the sweetest delicacy. Grace returned his kiss with the same passion. She knew, probably more than he did, just how close she'd come to losing everything in one night. Her life. Her man. Even his life had been in danger.

She felt his hardness pressed against her, and even there, in the parking lot, Grace knew she and Kenzo came close to never having this moment. When they broke the kiss, Kenzo and Grace were both panting. Kenzo held Grace to him, placing his forehead on hers.

After a moment, Kenzo took Grace's chin in his hand to look in her eyes. Grace winced, the pain of the cut from Anika's slaps finally breaking through the adrenaline." For the last fifteen years, Grace was responsible only for herself. She could defend herself with or without a weapon. But in this moment, in Kenzo's arms, she felt safer, more protected than she ever had in her life. She looked into Kenzo's eyes and saw pure love. Kenzo caressed her cheek, "Baby, she hurt you?" It was more statement than question, because Kenzo could see the cut and the purple bruise forming against her cheek. "Let me get you out of here, Love. Let me take care of you."

Things moved rather quickly in the weeks after the arrests of Anika and Amir Hassem as well as the men and women at the auction. The scandal of prominent businessmen being arrested for participating in a modern-day slave auction made national news, and Grace juggled press requests and building a rock-solid case. The rescued girls and women were given assistance and, in some cases, political asylum. Zara's betrayal of the unit was suppressed, so that she could be buried with honors and that her mother could receive her life insurance and survivor benefits. The team agreed that Zara's family had suffered enough.

Grace took another sip of her Argentinian Malbec. She'd nestled herself on the sofa as Kenzo had instructed while he fixed dinner. Her day had been filled with depositions and legal maneuverings for which she had no patience. Since their return from the Coast, Grace had practically moved into Kenzo's house, spending every night in each other's arms. Grace shivered when she thought about how tender and passionate their nights were. Grace was even beginning to like jazz, especially Miles Davis and John Coltrane, but she was able to get Kenzo to listen to a few blues records. Tonight, she was introducing him to the KPH Band. The lead singer was from Jackson, and she was thinking of hiring the band to perform for the annual Noelle Project benefit next year. Grace surveyed her surroundings at that thought and marveled at how easily such a thought came to her. Somehow, Noelle, a woman she'd never met and who had been the wife of the man she now loved completely, was as important to her as if she'd known her all her life. *Who would have thought?*

Kenzo interrupted her thoughts when he called her name. "Come to the dining room, Love." Grace thought that was odd since most of the time they ate either in the kitchen or the den.

"Coming," she called to him. She paused the track and headed for the dining room. Grace was weak when she entered the dining room. Kenzo had placed lit candles all around the room for a romantic dinner. The table had been decorated with white roses and lights that reminded her of the first time they saw each other. Kenzo was standing at the table and came toward her with an outstretched hand. He escorted her to her seat.

"I thought we could eat in here tonight...if that's okay."

"Of course." Grace smiled at him, and Kenzo thought his heart would stop. She took a whiff of dinner and laughed, "I know you didn't."

Her laughter was contagious, and Kenzo knew she'd figured out the menu. "I did."

He unveiled the tops of the dishes, and Grace clapped. "Oxtails!"

Kenzo looked sheepish, "Well, I did promise that I'd make them when you got back. And I keep my promises." He took her hand and blessed the food as he always did, and Grace realized how blessed she was to be here, at this table, with this man.

After a lovely dinner of oxtails and all the trimmings, Kenzo and Grace lapsed into a comfortable silence. Grace rose to clear the table, and Kenzo grabbed her hand.

"Leave them. They'll wait. I won't." Kenzo pulled a black velvet box from his pocket and lowered himself on one knee.

Grace stood there, stunned. "Kenzo," she whispered.

Kenzo stared into Grace's eyes and said, "Grace, I love you more than I ever imagined I could ever love again. Until you, I believed that I was unworthy of love, but you taught me that I deserved love, that I deserved you, Grace. You captured my heart and soul from the moment I saw you, and I promise that you'll have my heart and soul for the rest of my life. I promise I will spend the rest of my life loving you and making you the happiest woman in the world. Grace Harrington, will you do me the honor of becoming my wife and the mother of my children? Will you marry me?"

Kenzo slipped the ring on her finger. He'd designed the three-carat cushion cut ring with diamonds around the band. He insisted on flawless diamonds.

Tears sprang to Grace's eyes. "Oh, Kenzo." The ring twinkled even in the low light of the dining room but it was his eyes she saw and would always see. "I love you, too. Yes, I will marry you."

Kenzo stood up, and Grace threw her arms around his neck and kissed him. The kiss was sweet and passionate. Kenzo scooped her up in his arms and headed for the stairs, overcome with happiness and desire. With Grace curled into his arms, Kenzo whispered in her ear between kisses, "My Grace." He ascended the stairs to his bedroom where he would make love to his Grace all night.

Starting right now, Kenzo vowed to do everything in his power to give Grace the life she deserved for the rest of their lives.

CHAPTER 16

Kenzo and Grace decided to marry in September. Of course, Mama Hattie was adamant that the ceremony be at her church; she didn't care where the reception was held. But her only granddaughter was going to be married properly as she said, "in the house of the Lord right there on Ridgeway Street." Kenzo and Grace knew better than to object but exchanged glances. Mama Hattie didn't have to know that they had already decided the same but would have a grand reception at the historic King Edward Building.

Grace couldn't believe how quickly everything came together. The wedding party was small by design, consisting of their parents and Teresa, Treasure as Maid of Honor, and Riley as Best Man. Riley offered up his nieces and nephews as flower girls and ring bearers, which completed the circle. Grace knew Treasure would soldier through any events with Riley, but she couldn't believe that Kenzo was still oblivious to the attraction between the two.

Since Kenzo wanted to marry quickly, he gave Grace ninety days to plan the wedding. She could have anything she wanted, just please, he begged, do it in ninety days. She'd hired the best wedding planning team in Jackson, Lee and Molden Designs, to help her. When Grace conducted a final check of the ballroom, she gasped at the wonderland of lights and inhaled the scents of jasmine and vanilla wafting from the orchids. The sight brought tears to her eyes, the lights reminding her of the first night she saw Kenzo almost a year ago.

Kenzo stood in the front of the church and adjusted his tie. He looked at his parents, Grace's mother and grandmother, and Teresa, who was dabbing her eyes. Kenzo took a deep breath and exhaled slowly. Thank you, God, he thought. When the double doors opened, Kenzo's knees almost buckled. Grace was a vision in white lace. Grace selected a mermaid style dress that highlighted all of her curves but was southern conservative with a hint of bosom. The dress's sweeping train was covered in lace applique, as were the sleeves. She was his. His Grace. And soon she would be his wife.

Grace and Kenzo's eyes met as she entered the church, and she saw no one else but him. Her father, Colonel William Garner Harrington, dressed in his military blues, squeezed her hand. "Ready?" Grace didn't need to look at her father to respond because she couldn't pull her eyes away from Kenzo's if she tried. She whispered. "Yes, sir." As she and her father walked down the aisle, she smiled at the man waiting for her. Her father kissed her cheek. "I love you, sweetheart." Through tears, Grace looked up, "Love you too Daddy." Colonel Harrington looked at Kenzo and extended his hand. Kenzo and Colonel Harrington shook hands, and, in those seconds, a silent agreement passed between the two men about the precious woman standing between them.

Kenzo took Grace's hand, and she felt the heat between them, and any nervousness she felt melted away. Kenzo whispered in her ear, "You look beautiful, Love." Grace let his voice wash over her like silk. Grace knew she would never tire of hearing his voice or the proclamations of his love.

When they kneeled to pray, Kenzo held her hand tightly and rubbed the back of her hand with his thumb. The minister hadn't finished the sentence, "You may now kiss the bride" before Kenzo swept Grace into his arms and kissed her sweetly and passionately. Whistles and applause made them take a breath. Grace whispered to Kenzo, "I love you."

The reception was a roaring party when Riley rose from his seat to begin the toasts to the couple. Every person in the reception hall held their breath, because no one could ever guess what would come out of his mouth. Everyone knew that the consummate bachelor wasn't too keen on the institution of marriage. Yet he'd performed his best man duties to the fullest, including an epic bachelor party in New Orleans that was simply now referred to as the "Weekend."

Yet, Riley would surprise them all. No one knew how watching Kenzo fall in love again after so many years, watching his pain and sacrifice, and then to see the way he and Grace simply looked at each other had affected him. Riley made sure that the waitstaff had filled everyone's glasses with champagne before he began.

"I've known Kenzo over half my life, and I'm honored that he asked me to be his Best Man on this special day. As a friend and business partner, I know Kenzo as determined, focused, and sometimes, overbearing, especially when you come in a little late for a meeting on Monday morning." Riley faked coughed while the audience laughed when Kenzo rolled his eyes.

"But I digress," Riley continued. "Kenzo, my brother, we've been through some good times and some hard ones." Riley paused and everyone noted the change in his tone. "And I thought long and hard about what I would say today about losing my friend, but I realized that I didn't lose my friend. He was returned to me." Rlley turned to Grace, his voice cracking a little, "I didn't lose my friend, I gained two, and for that, my dear, I will be forever grateful."

Grace nodded at Riley through her tears, and Kenzo kissed the back of her hand and rubbed her back. Riley, then, turned to the audience and said, "And as the great philosopher Lao-Tzu once wrote, 'Being deeply loved by someone gives you strength, while loving someone deeply gives you courage.' Kenzo and Grace have a love of strength and courage, and it has been an honor to witness the fullness of their love. We should all be so blessed to find a love like theirs." Riley raised his glass, and everyone stood up, "To the Bride and Groom!"

"To the Bride and Groom!"

Kenzo nodded at his friend, visibly moved by the toast while Grace blew him a kiss of thanks. As the party resumed, Kenzo whispered in Grace's ear. "May I have this dance, Mrs. Dallas?"

Grace smiled at her husband. Her husband. *Lord, only You knew.* "Yes, Mr. Dallas, you may."

Kenzo led Grace to the dance floor just as the band started a rendition of "In a Sentimental Mood" and swept Grace into his arms, kissing her. "Do we have to stay much longer, Mrs. Dallas?" Grace could feel his desire for her, and she felt that burn grow within her.

Grace kissed him, "Just a couple more hours, Husband, and then I'm all yours. I promise."

Kenzo pulled her in closer and whispered in her ear. "I'm going to hold you to that for the rest of our lives."

——— THE END ———

EPILOGUE

Treasure lifted her glass and took a sip. She needed something stronger than champagne right now. She'd made it through months of avoiding Riley, but the nearness of him today was killing her. She barely survived the rehearsal dinner last night. Then today, the pictures. The ceremony. And now, Riley was standing there looking fine as hell in a tailor-made Armani tuxedo, making her swoon right there. She needed some air. Just as she rose to step out, she heard one of the wedding planners call all the single women for the bouquet toss.

Damn. Treasure couldn't catch a break today. She put on her best smile and walked to the front. There was a literal throng of single women positioning themselves to catch the bouquet. Treasure laughed at them. She'd long given up on that proposition, but these women were serious. Shoes had been cast aside, and Treasure thought she saw one woman crack her neck. Treasure saw Grace survey the crowd and look in her direction. Treasure knew that bouquet was coming like a missile in her direction.

Grace turned her back to the women. "One. Two. Three." Grace threw the bouquet and flicked her wrist so that the bouquet would veer to the right where Treasure was. Treasure saw the bouquet in the air, and *God help me,* she thought, she wanted it in that very moment. She reached up and pulled that bouquet out of the air, slightly nudging Nicholette Fredericks out of the way. Well, more like a push, but Nicholette had already been married twice...or was it three times, Treasure mused, as Nicholette picked herself up from the floor.

Grace thought she would never stop laughing.

When Kenzo got up to do the garter toss, not a man joined him. Marcus and Rlley were making air signals of "NO WAY," but the planners were rounding up every single man in the room and physically dragging them to the dance floor. Kenzo laughed at his friends, who now all looked like they were sentenced to the principal's office.

Kenzo addressed his crew, "C'mon, guys, let's get this done. Then you can go back to your single lives. It's for the ladies, particularly mine." Kenzo winked at them before turning around. He heard their grumbles, and he laughed.

"One. Two. Three." Kenzo threw the garter haphazardly. He nearly choked when he realized that Rlley had the garter. Riley looked mortified.

Kenzo slapped him on the back. "Well, look at it this way. You'll get to dance with Treasure."

Riley groaned, "Whatever, man." But Riley heard Treasure's laugh above the others' in the room. She was standing with Grace, holding her bouquet and smiling, and Riley stopped short at the sight of her. The candlelight danced across her features and she looked like a goddess in the silver gown she wore. She was the most beautiful woman he'd ever seen, and that weekend between them flooded his senses. Kenzo had joined the laughter between the two women, and Rlley didn't hear a word. All he heard, all he saw, was Treasure's eyes, her mouth, her smile.

Rlley heard a voice that he vaguely recognized as his. "Would you like to dance, Treasure?" He held his hand out for hers, and Treasure stared at it and then at him. Treasure looked at Grace, who simply smiled at her and nodded.

As Treasure took Riley's hand, she stopped him, "You don't have to do this."

Riley looked at Treasure. "Yes, I do."

ABOUT THE AUTHOR

C.L. Jackson lives in Jackson, Mississippi. She loves being a southern belle and clutching her pearls when the need arises. *Deserving Grace* is her debut novel.

Made in the USA
Columbia, SC
06 December 2019